SPECTRE COLLECTORS

TOO GHOUL FOR SCHOOL

SPECTRE COLLECTORS

TOO GHOUL FOR SCHOOL

BARRY HUTCHISON

nosy crow

First published 2017 by Nosy Crow Ltd
The Crow's Nest, 14 Baden Place, Crosby Row
London SE1 1YW, UK
www.nosycrow.com

ISBN: 978 0 85763 960 8

Nosy Crow and associated logos are trademarks
and/or registered trademarks of Nosy Crow Ltd

A CIP catalogue record for this book is available from the British Library.

Printed and bound in the UK by Clays Ltd, St Ives Plc.
Typeset by Tiger Media

Papers used by Nosy Crow are made from wood grown in
sustainable forests.

3 5 7 9 8 6 4 2

For Michael Lopez,
co-founder of the original
Spectre Collectors. I hope
you're still having grand
adventures, old friend.

B. H.

CHAPTER 1

Denzel Edgar was halfway through some particularly unpleasant maths homework when he saw the ghost.

He'd barely taken out his workbook when he first felt the icy tingle down his spine. He was sharpening his pencil when all the fine hairs on the back of his neck stood on end. Denzel looked around to find where the draught was coming from, but every window and door was shut tight.

He was wrestling with a head-wrecking bit of algebra when his eraser jumped out of his pencil case and flopped on to the dining room table. Denzel stopped writing and looked at the rectangular rubber with its graphite-stained ends. He looked at his pencil case. Then, with a shrug, he placed the eraser back inside.

A moment later, it hopped out again. This time, Denzel didn't move to return the rubber to the case. Instead, he just stared at it, wondering quietly what was going on. As he stared, his breath formed wispy white clouds in front of his face. It reminded him of being outside in December, only he was inside. And it was June.

Denzel's whole body began to shiver. He felt cold from the inside out, but he felt something even more troubling, too.

He felt like he was not alone.

"Wh-who's there?" he whispered. The words sounded smothered by the suffocating silence of the house. He heard nothing, saw nothing, but felt … something. A tickle of movement across his face and through his hair, as if the air itself were taking form around him, becoming something different, something more.

Down on the tabletop, Denzel's eraser stood on end. It walked towards him, rocking from side to side the way his dads would walk the wardrobe from one end of his bedroom to the other whenever they took it upon themselves to reorganise the place. Unlike the wardrobe, though, the rubber was walking all on its own.

Instinctively, Denzel slapped his hand down on the

waddling eraser. He felt it squirm in his grip as he forced it back into the pencil case and zipped it inside. The pencil case twitched and wriggled, so Denzel slammed his schoolbag down on top, and quickly backed away from the table.

He could feel his heart beating at the back of his throat. His dads wouldn't be home for another hour or more. He was all alone in the house.

So why couldn't he shake the feeling that he wasn't?

And then he saw it, reflected in the glass of a picture frame: a dark shape lingering in the corner of the dining room, spreading up the walls and across the ceiling like a nasty case of rot.

At first, Denzel tried to convince himself he'd imagined it. The dark thing behind him wasn't real. It couldn't be real. He was going mad, obviously. That last equation had fractured his poor overworked brain, making him see ... whatever that thing was.

He knew if he could just summon the courage to turn round he'd find nothing there but the empty wall. Maybe there'd be a shadow or something, but nothing like the writhing tangle of smoky black tendrils that was currently reflected back at him.

Slowly – ever so slowly – Denzel turned. As he did, he closed both his eyes, so by the time he was facing the corner, he was still none the wiser as to whether anything was actually there.

He wanted his eyes to open, but his eyes were having none of it. It took several deep breaths and a whispered pep talk before his right eye relented. His left one, however, remained fully committed to staying shut.

To Denzel's dismay, when he opened his eye he saw that the corner wasn't empty. The thing that lurked there looked like a cross between an octopus and a chimney fire. It was as black and intangible as smoke, with six or seven long tentacles all tangled in knots. The shape seemed to pulse in time with Denzel's crashing heartbeat, getting faster and faster as Denzel's panic bubbled up inside him.

One of the thing's tentacles reached out for him, and Denzel stumbled back. He raced for the door leading into the hall and pulled it open. The tentacle whipped past him, slamming the door again and holding it shut.

Denzel ducked and scanned the room, searching for something to defend himself with. The best he could find was a little plastic model of the Blackpool Tower that a neighbour had brought them back from holiday. It wasn't the ideal weapon with which to battle a malevolent supernatural entity, Denzel suspected, but it was the only one he had.

"S-stay back!" he said, thrusting the Blackpool Tower towards the smoke thing, pointy-end first. "I'm w-warning you."

One of the smoky tendrils lashed out. A snow globe – another holiday memento – exploded against the wall above Denzel, showering him in glass, glitter and a tiny reproduction of Edinburgh Castle.

Yelping in fright, Denzel covered his head, just as a dining chair flipped into the air and slammed down beside him with a *smash*. Denzel dived for the door again, but the tendril still had it held closed.

The window! It was Denzel's only chance of escape. Waving the Blackpool Tower in what he hoped was a vaguely threatening way, he leapt over the broken dining chair and raced towards the window. He was making a grab for the cord that would pull up the blinds when the whole thing exploded inwards, knocking him off his feet and on to the dining table.

Denzel's momentum carried him over the polished tabletop. As he slid off the other side, the table tipped, shielding him from the smoke thing – and whatever had blown his window to bits.

Cautiously, Denzel poked the top of his head above the table edge, just enough to give him a view of the room. Two figures stepped through the gap where the window and part of the wall used to be. It was hard to make them out through the cloud of plaster dust, but from their silhouettes it looked like the bigger of the two was carrying an assault rifle.

Denzel looked at the small plastic Blackpool Tower he'd somehow managed to keep hold of during his short flight across the room. After a moment's consideration, he quietly set it down on the floor.

"Scanning for hostile," barked the figure with the gun. It was a man, that was all Denzel could figure out. Young-ish, he thought, but he couldn't be sure. He jabbed his little finger in his ear, trying to clear out the ringing noise from the explosion. Someone must have heard the sound. Help would be on its way. With a bit of luck, no one would kill him before it arrived.

"Any sign?" asked the other figure. This one was a teenage girl, Denzel reckoned, and sounded far less confident than her partner.

"Can't pinpoint it," the man said, and something about his voice this time told Denzel he was a teenager, too. A red light blinked on the barrel of his gun, as he slowly circled on the spot. "But it's here."

Denzel glanced over to the corner. The black shape was still there, pulsing and twisting as before. He found himself gesturing towards it with his eyes, trying to draw the strangers' attention to it without being noticed himself.

"Perhaps the Third Eye of Sherm will shed some light on the situation!" the girl said grandly. Denzel heard the boy sigh as his partner began to mumble below her breath. The room was still one big cloud of white dust, but through the fog Denzel saw a shape illuminate in purple light on the girl's forehead. It was an oval with a circle in the middle, like a child's drawing of an eye.

"The Third Eye of Sherm!" boomed the girl, in a voice that rolled around the room. When the echo faded, the boy gave a disapproving tut.

"Do you have to do that every time?"

"Yes," said the girl. "It's tradition."

"It's dumb," the boy replied. "Besides, it blows our element of surprise."

The girl jabbed a thumb back towards the hole where the window had been. "Um... Hello? I'm not the one who obliterated the wall. The front door was literally five paces along the street."

"You have your traditions, I have mine," said the boy. "Whatever. Can you see it?"

"The Third Eye of Sherm sees all," said the girl.

"Yes, but does it see the hostile?"

The girl turned and scanned the room. The purple

glow of the eye on her forehead swept across the walls like a searchlight, passing right across the smoke-thing. "No," she admitted. "It doesn't see that. It can't be here."

The boy gave his gun a smack with the heel of his hand. The light flickered then came back on. "You sure? I'm definitely reading something."

"What do you trust more? Eight billion pounds of advanced tracking technology," began the girl. She tapped her forehead. "Or this baby?"

"Eight billion pounds of advanced tracking technology," said the boy, without hesitation.

Denzel wanted to scream to them that both the tracking technology and the fancy glowing eye were both rubbish, because the "hostile", as they called it, was right there in the corner of the room, just sort of hanging about looking ominous.

He watched both figures turn around another couple of times, each carrying out their own search. He'd expected to hear sirens by now, but there seemed to be no sound at all coming in through the hole in the wall. It was almost 5pm. The street should be filled with the teatime rush.

Denzel glanced over to the dark shape in the corner, and suddenly got the feeling that it was looking back at him. It had no eyes, but he could feel its gaze drilling into him, piercing right down into his soul.

"Oh well. False alarm, I guess," said the girl. The dust cloud was settling, and Denzel could just make out that she wore a dark-red robe with what looked to be ridiculously wide shoulder-pads. She wiped a hand across her forehead, and the glowing eye disappeared. "Let us slip away like the Shadows of Shak'tee!" she said, making an elaborate gesture with her hands.

The boy looked her up and down. "What was that meant to be?"

"Just something I'm trying out," the girl replied, sounding a little embarrassed. "I thought it'd make me appear more, you know, *mysterious*."

"It makes you appear deranged," the boy said. "Come on, let's go."

Denzel felt his stomach tighten as the two figures turned back towards the hole in the wall. The dark cloud began to throb more quickly, and Denzel could almost sense its excitement. Soon it would have him all to itself, and Denzel got the feeling that was just what it wanted.

"Wait, d-don't leave!" Denzel yelped. He pointed to the corner, where the dark thing now twisted into knots. "It's there. It's right there!"

The two figures turned sharply, the girl raising her hands in front of her, the boy taking aim at Denzel with his weapon. They stepped closer and Denzel got his first clear look at them as they emerged from the cloud of dust.

He had thought the girl was wearing a robe, but could see now it was a flowing red cape draped over a dark-green tunic. A belt of gold-coloured rope was tied around her middle, and there were more rings on her fingers than in a jeweller's shop window. She looked younger than Denzel had been expecting – fourteen, maybe, possibly even thirteen like him.

The boy beside her was a little older, but not much. He was dressed in a military uniform, but not one from any army Denzel had ever seen. The camouflage pattern on the outfit was made up of shades of silver and blue, with shiny blue boots that reached halfway up his shins. Not really the ideal colours for hiding in bushes, Denzel thought. His sleeves were rolled up, and his gloved hands gripped the stock and barrel of his weapon, which Denzel was somewhat dismayed to note was pointing at his head.

The boy's eyes narrowed, then he shot the girl a sideways glance. "Third Eye of Sherm sees everything, does it?"

"Well your scanners didn't pick him up, either!" the girl protested.

SPECTRE COLLECTORS

"Duck!" shouted Denzel, as an *I've Been to Legoland Windsor* ceramic plate whistled through the air towards the intruders. The boy reacted quickly, ducking just before the plate hit him. The girl wasn't so lucky.

"Ow!" she yelped, as the plate smashed against the back of her head. "That really hurt!"

"Where is it?" demanded the boy, spinning in the direction the plate had come from.

"There!" Denzel cried, pointing to the corner again.

"He can't possibly see it," the girl protested, gingerly touching the back of her head. "I mean… You can't, can you?"

"Great big black cloud thing!" Denzel yelped. "Lots of tentacles. It's literally right there in front of you!"

The boy raised his weapon. "I'll take your word for it," he said.

He squeezed the trigger. A piercing squeal filled the room.

And everything in Denzel's world went white.

CHAPTER 2

When the light faded, the black shape was nowhere to be seen. The boy *clacked* a switch on the side of his weapon and a hand grenade-sized red gemstone dropped from the bottom. The girl bent low to catch it before it hit the floor, then hurriedly wrapped it in what looked like the thin branch of a tree, muttering as she fumbled with the knot.

"Bullseye," crowed the boy. "Boom!" He turned to Denzel, his satisfied grin quickly turning to a cold stare of suspicion. "You knew where it was. How?"

Denzel got to his feet, kneading his eyes with his finger and thumb. The glow of the light was still burned into his retinas, and when he blinked the usual darkness had been replaced by a shimmering white fog.

"I could see it," Denzel said.

"You could *see it*?" snorted the boy, looking him slowly up and down. "How could you see it?"

"I just sort of pointed my eyes in its general direction, and there it was," Denzel said. "How could you not see it? It wasn't exactly difficult."

"No, not difficult," agreed the girl, slipping the bound gemstone into a small leather bag that hung from her belt. "*Impossible*. You can't see poltergeists. It can't be done."

Denzel shrugged. "Well, maybe it wasn't a polter-thingy, then."

"Polter*geist*. And of course it was!" said the girl. She glanced at the boy. "I mean... It was, wasn't it?"

"Sensors said so," the boy replied.

"Well, yes, but ... that doesn't prove anything. They're not exactly reliable."

"More reliable than your stupid magic eye."

The girl gasped. "How *dare* you doubt the Third Eye of Sherm?"

Denzel left them to their bickering and gazed around at what was left of the dining room. The gaping hole in the wall was the worst of it, of course, but there was plenty of other damage, too.

The top part of the table had come away from the base, and at least two of its chairs were in pieces. The display cabinet where the crockery was kept had been knocked over, and most of the plates lay smashed on the floor.

The carpet was thick with dust, splinters of wood and shards of glass, and there was an oval scorch mark on the wall where the smoke-thing had been.

"My dads are going to kill me," Denzel mumbled. He turned to the intruders, suddenly angry. "Who are you two? What right do you have to come in here and trash my house?"

"We've got every right," snapped the boy, jabbing a finger right up in Denzel's face. "That was a Class Eight hostile apparition. Left unchecked it could've done all kinds of damage."

Denzel gestured around at his dining room, just as the lampshade fell from the ceiling and shattered on the floor. "And what, you thought you'd give it a hand?"

The boy stepped forward so he was leaning over Denzel. Denzel held his ground, trying not to show how much his legs were shaking.

"Yeah, but the difference is it doesn't tidy up after itself," the boy said. "Unlike us."

SPECTRE COLLECTORS

He eyeballed Denzel for a few seconds. Denzel stared back, trying not to flinch.

The boy unclipped a walkie-talkie from his belt, but the girl put a hand on his wrist to stop him and smiled hopefully. "Wait, can I try?"

The boy sighed. "Not this again."

"I've got it this time, I've totally nailed it. Promise. Just let me try."

The boy glanced at Denzel, then at his partner. He shook his head, but lowered the radio. "Fine. Whatever. Do it. But be quick."

The girl clapped her hands excitedly, then stepped back. "OK," she mumbled. "Here goes. This is it. This time there's no stopping—"

"Get a move on," the boy snapped.

"Right. Yes. Here goes."

Denzel watched as the girl's fingers danced and weaved through the air. As she waggled her digits, she chanted. It sounded like gibberish to Denzel, but after a moment the girl's fingertips began to sparkle and shimmer.

Lowering her hands, she turned to the gap in the wall. "Here we go," she whispered. "It's going to work this time. I can feel it. It's going to work."

Denzel leaned left and right, trying to see out through the hole. "What's going to work?" he asked.

"Just wait. Any minute now," said the girl. "Any minute…" She squealed with excitement. "There! Look!"

Denzel watched as a grey squirrel hopped in through the damaged wall. It stopped on the carpet and peered around the room, its nose twitching. A moment later, two sparrows fluttered in, carrying something between them.

"Is that… Is that a duster?" Denzel asked.

"Yes!" the girl shrieked. She hopped excitedly from foot to foot as a stag ducked its antlers through the gap and trotted into the room, clutching a broom in its mouth. "It's working! It's actually working!"

"Great," said the boy flatly.

The girl grinned from ear to ear as a family of ducks waddled into the room, carrying a number of power tools between them. "Brace yourself," she yelped. "This is going to be the most magical clean-up *ever*!"

Three minutes later, the dining room had descended into chaos. The sparrows were pecking at the stag's eyes, while it kicked the remaining dining chairs to pieces and tried to use its antlers to make kebabs of the ducks.

Two badgers, who had arrived late, were taking it in turns to rough up the squirrel. The squirrel, however, had managed to get its hands on a can of furniture polish, and it chittered angrily as it sprayed the badgers in the face.

Denzel watched the carnage unfolding in horror. Beside him, the girl in the cloak scratched her head. "This didn't happen to Snow White." She sighed. "Oh well, back to the drawing board."

She dodged a duck and ducked the deer, then turned to the boy and offered him a shaky smile. "Maybe you should do the honours, after all."

"Oh, you think?" the boy said, reaching for his radio. "Domestic clean-up needed at this location." He turned to Denzel. "How long until your parents get home?"

Denzel's stomach knotted at the thought of it. "It depends on traffic and stuff, but – I don't know – twenty minutes?" he said.

The boy muttered something below his breath then raised the radio to his mouth again. "Priority one. Get here now."

There was a crackled confirmation from the other end of the line, and the boy returned the walkie-talkie to his belt clip. He and the girl both rounded on Denzel, just as the stag grabbed the broom in its mouth and set about trying to mash the sparrows into a feathery paste.

"This is madness," Denzel said, gawping at the mess. "This is, I mean… This is insane. Who *are* you people?"

"We're part of a top-secret organisation dedicated to protecting the human race from supernatural threats," said the girl. She sounded almost robotic, like she'd said the same words a hundred times before. "We go by many names. The Cult of Sh'grath. The Messengers of the Allwhere. The Seventh Army of the Enlightened."

The boy leaned in front of her. "But we prefer the *Spectre Collectors*."

Denzel frowned, trying his best to ignore the squirrel that came riding past his feet on the back of a baby duck. "The Spectre Collectors? So ... what? You catch ghosts?"

Both the girl and boy nodded. "Among other things," said the boy. "But like she said, it's top secret. Above top secret, in fact."

"So how come you're telling me?" asked Denzel, suddenly nervous.

The girl reached into another bag that was tied around her belt and took out a handful of something that looked like glitter. Unlike glitter, though, the air above it seemed to shimmer, like heat rising from a hot tarmac road.

"Because," said the boy. "You're not going to remember any of it."

Before Denzel could reply, the girl blew on the dust. It swirled into a miniature tornado, then hit Denzel full in the face. He coughed and spluttered as he felt it flutter up his nose. It tickled his sinuses, like a sneeze that was sulking and refusing to come out.

"What did you do to me?" he demanded, then he looked down at the table in front of him.

His homework was there, open at a particularly brain-frying piece of algebra. He stared at it for a long time, before realising he'd already filled in the answer. He felt like he could almost remember writing it, but it was slipping away from him like a dream.

He got up from the table and walked to the window. The blinds were open and he could see the street outside. His dads' car was pulling up, and Denzel felt his stomach rumble. It was Wednesday, which meant takeaway night.

"Please let it be Chinese, please let it be Chinese," he whispered, crossing his fingers. He pushed his chair back in and made for the door leading to the hall.

Halfway there, he felt something crunch underfoot. Denzel bent and picked up a tangle of broken plastic.

"Huh," he said, turning a tiny Blackpool Tower over in his hands. "How did that get there?"

He set the broken trinket back on its shelf, took a lingering look around the neat and tidy room, then headed through to join his parents for dinner.

CHAPTER 3

Next morning, with his mouth still burning from the night before's tasty-yet-ultimately-disappointing Indian, Denzel set off for school.

As ever, he had his morning journey planned out to the exact minute. At exactly eight thirty-eight he would leave the house, remembering to wave to old Mrs Grigor across the road. At eight thirty-nine, he'd start walking towards the bus stop up near the shops. At eight forty, the bus would roar past him as if he wasn't there. Eight forty-one to five past nine would then be spent running frantically to school, and trying not to vomit from the effort.

SPECTRE COLLECTORS

It was the same routine every morning, and today was no different. His registration teacher, Mr Gavistock, barely batted an eyelid when he clattered in, puffing and wheezing and on the brink of passing out.

"Here, sir," Denzel offered, flopping down in his chair. The moment his bottom touched the plastic, the bell rang. Everyone else got to their feet and bustled out of the classroom.

"Ooh. Sorry, Denzel," said Mr Gavistock. He sucked on his grey moustache, his pen hovering just millimetres above the register. "The bell went before I could mark you as present. You'll have to pick up a late slip from the office."

Denzel glanced at the register. "Can't you mark me here now?"

Mr Gavistock slowly set his pen down and leaned forwards, his hands clasped in front of him. "No, Denzel. Because that would be against the rules."

"Yeah, but it's only a few seconds. And I made it before the bell went."

Mr Gavistock drew in a long breath. "But I hadn't marked you present when it rang, Denzel," he said. "My hands are tied."

"But—"

"My hands are tied, Denzel," said the teacher. "You

understand what I mean by that phrase? My hands are tied."

Denzel stood up and hoisted his bag on to his shoulder. "Yeah, but, I mean... They aren't, are they?" he said. "You could just mark me down. No one would really care."

Mr Gavistock arched an eyebrow. "I could," he admitted. Then he flicked his tongue across his 'tache and smirked. "But where would be the fun in that?"

As a result of having to go to the office to pick up a late slip, Denzel was fifteen minutes late for maths. Mr Gavistock, who was also Denzel's maths teacher, looked disappointed at him when he stumbled in.

"Twice in one day, Denzel," the teacher said, shaking his head. "And I'm guessing you haven't done your homework, either."

"I have, actually," Denzel said. He fished around in his schoolbag, then pulled out a crumpled sheet of paper. Smoothing it against his chest, he handed the sheet to the teacher.

Mr Gavistock waved Denzel over to his seat and scanned the page. "Amazingly, this all looks to be right," he said. "How did you manage that?"

Denzel sat down at his desk and rummaged in his bag for his pencil case. "Um... Just thought about it."

Mr Gavistock raised a bushy eyebrow. "You 'just

thought about it'?"

Denzel nodded. The truth was, he couldn't really remember how he'd managed to solve the homework equations. He had absolutely no recollection of doing them.

"So what you really mean is you copied it from the Internet," Mr Gavistock said. He raised a long, bony finger and tick-tocked it from side to side. "Tut-tut. Disappointing, Denzel." He slowly tore the sheet in half. "Very disappointing."

Denzel knew there was no point in protesting. Algebra wasn't his strong point – he hadn't yet figured out what his strong point actually was, but it definitely wasn't that – and as he had no memory of doing the equations, he couldn't offer much of a counter-argument.

Besides, the worksheet was already in at least eight pieces, so there was no coming back for it. He decided to keep his mouth shut and just get on with the day.

The rest of the morning passed in much the same way as every school day did – slowly, and with an overwhelming sense of disappointment.

At lunchtime, Denzel sat on his usual spot on the usual wall, waiting for his best friend, Smithy, to turn up. As usual.

Smithy wasn't in any of Denzel's classes, but they'd

been friends since the first day of secondary school, and met up at lunchtime every day so they could hang out and avoid having to talk to anyone else.

"What you got today, then?" asked Smithy. He spoke in a high-pitched nasal whine, thanks to some sinus problem he never grew tired of talking about in stomach-churning detail. He hopped up and sat on the wall beside Denzel.

Denzel opened his lunch box and peeled back the top layer of his sandwich. "Pastrami, dill pickle and Emmental," he said. "On wholegrain. What about you?"

Smithy pulled a crumpled, slightly soggy brown paper bag from somewhere deep in his schoolbag. He opened it and gave it an experimental sniff. "Scrambled egg." He looked hopefully at Denzel's sandwich. "Wanna swap?"

"Not really," said Denzel.

"Nah, nor me," agreed Smithy.

Denzel gestured to his sandwich. "Want a bit?"

"Go on, then," Smithy nodded. He reached into Denzel's lunchbox and lifted out one half of the sandwich. Setting it on top of his lumpy paper bag, he proceeded to carefully remove the pickle and pastrami, then tossed them both away.

"Cheers," he said, taking a bite of the now cheese-only sandwich.

SPECTRE COLLECTORS

They sat in silence for a while, munching on their lunch. Denzel's feet were on the ground, while Smithy's dangled several centimetres above it.

"What would you rather fight, right?" Smithy began.

"Go on," said Denzel.

"A zombie with the brain of an evil genius, or an evil genius with the brain of a zombie?"

Denzel chewed thoughtfully. "An evil genius with the brain of a zombie," he decided.

"How come?"

"Because he's not really an evil genius any more, is he?"

"Yes he is. He's an evil genius with the brain of a zombie," said Smithy.

"That's exactly my point," Denzel said. "A zombie with the brain of an evil genius is a super-intelligent unkillable monster who wants to rule the world. An evil genius with the brain of a zombie is just a normal zombie. He'll just shuffle about a bit moaning and trying to eat people."

Smithy nodded. "Fair enough," he said. He reached into his paper bag and scooped out a handful of cold scrambled egg. "Want some?" he offered.

Denzel screwed up his sandwich wrapper. "Nah, you're all right," he said. He nodded at a bin near the wall six or seven metres along from them. "How much will you give me if I get this in?"

"A million pounds," Smithy said, cramming the sloppy egg into his mouth.

Denzel shook his head. "That's too much. That's mad."

"Oh, OK." Smithy said. He shrugged. "One pound?"

"That's better," Denzel said, shutting one eye. He held the rolled up ball of cellophane between finger and thumb and moved it back and forth like a darts player taking aim.

"And Denzel Edgar lines up the shot," Smithy said in a hushed whisper. "All eyes are on him now. Just one throw stands between him and a victory that's sure to go down in history as one of the all-time pinnacles of human achievement. Edgar holds his breath. He aims. He throws…"

The ball of plastic wrap curved through the air, bounced once on the rim of the bin, then dropped inside.

Smithy jumped down and thrust his arms into the air. "He makes the shot! The crowd goes wild! Truly, they may as well all drop dead now, safe in the knowledge that they've witnessed the single greatest moment in all of human history, as young Denzel Edgar takes—"

The ball of plastic landed beside Smithy with a soft *paff*. He stopped cheering and looked down at it. "Oh, I take that back," he said. "You missed."

SPECTRE COLLECTORS

Denzel hopped down and picked up the cling film wad. "It came back out," he said, frowning. "That's weird." Taking a step closer, he tossed it underarm into the bin. He held up a hand to stop Smithy launching into another celebration.

They both watched the bin for what felt like quite a long time. "What are we waiting for?" Smithy whispered.

Denzel relaxed. "Nothing. I don't know. I just thought—"

The ball leapt out again and rolled to a stop in front of Denzel. He and Smithy both looked down at it, then at each other, before finally turning their attention to the bin.

"Hello?" Denzel called. "Is there someone in there?"

A flattened Coke can spun up from inside the bin, then clattered on the ground. "Great. We've got a bin weirdo," Smithy muttered.

"What's a bin weirdo?"

"It's a receptacle for holding rubbish, *freak*," Smithy said. He grinned. "See what I did there? I deliberately misunderstood your initial question so— Wah!"

Smithy ducked as a torrent of litter exploded upwards out of the bin like lava from an erupting volcano. Cans and plastic bottles shot several metres into the air, then clattered to the ground around them. Crisp bags swirled on the breeze and floated down like autumn leaves.

Once all the rubbish had come to rest on the ground, Smithy turned to Denzel. "I think you broke the bin."

Down at their feet, the litter began to tremble. It vibrated across the tarmac, gathering in a spot just a few paces ahead of the boys. They both took a step back as the rubbish assembled itself into two piles, which both quickly grew upwards until they formed pillars just a little taller than Smithy and a little shorter than Denzel.

The pillars joined together and continued to grow upwards, forming one garbage-filled mass. As he stared, Denzel began to recognise the shape.

It was a person. Or a figure, at least. A ten-feet tall figure made of drinks cans, chocolate wrappers and half-eaten bits of fruit.

Smithy puffed out his cheeks. "There's something you don't see every day," he said.

"We should probably run," Denzel began. "I don't think—"

"DIE, RUBBISH-MONSTER!" Smithy hollered, swinging with his schoolbag as he launched himself at the towering figure's legs. The litter parted and he stumbled right through, hit the bin, then fell head-first inside.

"Should've run," Smithy called, his voice sounding echoey and muffled. "Totally misjudged that."

SPECTRE COLLECTORS

A hand, made largely of banana skins and Wotsits, grabbed for Denzel. He staggered back, swinging at it with his schoolbag. "Get off," he yelped.

The hand slammed down and Denzel dodged, barely avoiding being splattered against the ground. The mulchy stench of rot wafted up his nostrils, making him gag.

Smithy was still in the bin. The litter-thing didn't seem to have any interest in him, and was focusing all its attention on Denzel instead.

Denzel's heart crashed. The monster stepped closer on its teetering legs, and Denzel felt a tingle at the back of his mind, like the stirring of a long-forgotten memory.

"There is something awfully familiar about this," he whispered.

And then, he ran.

CHAPTER 4

Denzel hightailed it past the bike sheds, across the visitors' car park, and round the outside of the dining hall.

He was tearing across the little rectangle of concrete between the dining hall and the school's main entrance when the screaming started. His schoolmates scattered as the rubbish-thing skidded around the corner and chased Denzel down, its long litter legs bounding easily across the yard.

"Out of the way, watch out, coming through!" Denzel yelped, hopping and jigging through the throng of older girls who sat on the school's front steps. The girls tutted their annoyance at first, before launching into a chorus of panicky squeals when they spotted the towering trash-figure approaching.

Denzel clattered through the front door and stumbled into the reception area. The inner security doors were shut tight. He rattled on the handles, instantly incurring the wrath of the school secretary on the other side.

"Oi!" she said, rapping her knuckles on the glass. "Cut that out. Ring the buzzer like everyone else."

"Just open the flippin' doors!" Denzel yelped, glancing back over his shoulder. "Hurry up!"

The secretary crossed her arms. "Ring the buzzer," she said.

"Aaargh! OK!" Denzel cried. He fumbled with the button and a loud *BZZZZT* rang out. "There! Happy?"

The secretary touched the button that unlocked the door. "Yes," she said. "Wasn't so difficult, was—"

She screamed and staggered backwards as the outer doors were ripped from their hinges and the trash-creature ducked to fill the doorframe. Denzel yanked open the glass doors and scrambled through, just as the cheesy-corn-based-snack hand grabbed for him once again.

Hurtling along the corridor, Denzel dodged and shoved his way through throngs of pupils. Squeals and scuffles of panic started somewhere behind, and Denzel knew the monster was still coming for him. The panic quickly erupted into screaming hysteria, as everyone who was currently in the corridor decided they'd really rather not be.

Pupils ducked into doorways and dived through windows, desperately trying to get out of the path of the rampaging trash-beast. Denzel puffed and panted, tasting the thing's pungent scent with every rasping breath.

He skidded around the corner at the end of the corridor, and glanced back just long enough to see the monster bounding along on all fours, getting closer and closer and—

THWACK! It failed to turn in time and slammed into the wall at full speed. Denzel kept his distance as the creature collapsed in on itself, becoming once again just an unmoving mound of crisp bags and Coke cans.

Denzel watched the rubbish-heap closely, searching for any sign of movement. He was studying it so hard that he failed to notice a door open right beside it. Denzel jumped as Mr Gavistock exploded out of the room.

"What is the meaning of all this noise?" he demanded. He yelped as he slid on a half-eaten cheese and pickle sandwich, only just managing to stay upright.

SPECTRE COLLECTORS

The teacher gaped in horror at the rubbish heap, then rounded on Denzel, his bony finger wagging. "How dare you, Denzel? How *dare* you? Look at this mess! I am beside myself with rage. Do you understand what I mean by that phrase? Beside myself with rage!"

"Uh, yeah, but..." Denzel began, standing on his tiptoes to see over the teacher's shoulder.

"You never fail to disappoint, do you, Denzel?"

"No, but..."

"After this morning, I thought... Look me in the eye when I'm talking to you," Mr Gavistock barked. He jabbed his finger in Denzel's direction. "And where do you think you're going?" he demanded, as Denzel hurriedly began to back away. "Get back here this—"

WHAM! A scything arm made mostly of plastic bottles and Styrofoam trays smashed the teacher against the wall with a really quite surprising amount of force.

Denzel dashed down the corridor as Mr Gavistock slumped to the floor. The trash-monster finished pulling itself back together and the chase was on again. Denzel's legs ached. His heart pounded. He desperately needed the toilet. There was no doubt about it – this was shaping up to be one of his top five worst lunch breaks ever.

He turned another corner and saw the corridor ahead was jam-packed with kids. They sat on the floor and leaned against the walls, chatting and laughing, completely unaware of the enormous monster currently hurtling in their general direction.

There was no way Denzel was getting through that lot in a hurry. He skidded left and threw himself at the fire exit. Pushing down the bar, he stumbled outside. The alarm began to wail, but was promptly drowned out by the sound of a twenty-feet-tall garbage-beast exploding through the doorway behind him.

"Oh, come on!" Denzel groaned. All around him, his schoolmates stared in wonder, then screamed in terror. Denzel hurried through the criss-crossing mass of panicking bodies, heading for... where? He had no idea, he just knew he had to put as much distance as possible between himself and the trash-thing.

The school's side gates were dead ahead. There was a road out there, then a housing estate with a network of twisting back alleys. Maybe he could lose the monster in there.

Lowering his head, he raced for the exit, trying to block-out the thudding of the litter-thing's footsteps closing behind him. Denzel dodged past a smaller boy who appeared to be literally frozen to the spot in fear, and suddenly the gate was looming dead ahead.

With a final frantic push he forced his legs to move

faster. Keeping his head low, he threw himself towards the exit...

Then slammed hard into a patch of rock-solid thin air. Denzel stumbled backwards, clutching at his suddenly throbbing skull.

"Ow, ow, ow!" he grimaced, hopping from foot to foot. He squinted at the empty space in front of him. "What was that?"

He raised his arms in front of him and tried a more cautious jog forwards. Almost immediately, he hit an invisible wall. The outline of his handprints *fizzled* in the air, then vanished when he stepped back.

"What? But... I mean..." Denzel spluttered, but before he could work out what the end of that sentence was going to be, the stench of rotten fruit and chips was suddenly all around him.

Slowly, Denzel turned. He looked up.

And up.

And up.

The trash-monster loomed over him. It had given itself eyes made of ketchup-stained paper plates. It also had a Pringles tube where its nose should have been, but that could just have been a coincidence.

"Top *three* worst lunch breaks ever," Denzel whispered. There was nowhere to run now. Denzel could only wait for the thing to attack, and hope it didn't hurt too much.

But it didn't attack. It dropped to one knee, and bent low over him until the smell of rubbish made Denzel gag. "What... What do you want?" he choked, but before he could get an answer, the creature imploded. There was no big noise or epic fanfare to accompany it – one moment it was there, the next moment all its component parts had rushed to meet each other in the middle of its body.

The litter squashed together and compacted into a lumpy sphere, no bigger than a basketball. It fell to the ground with a hefty *thud*, and Denzel found himself looking down the barrel of a futuristic assault rifle.

A boy, just a little older than him, stood at the less-dangerous end of the weapon, squinting down the sights. He wore a blue and silver uniform with shiny blue boots. A girl in a colourful cape and tunic stood behind him. They both raised their eyebrows in surprise.

"You!" said the boy.

"You?" said the girl.

"Uh, yeah. Me," said Denzel. He looked at them both in turn. "I feel like I should be saying 'you', too, but I have no idea who you are," he babbled. He raised his hands. "Don't shoot, by the way."

There was a savage screech from a few metres away.

"Leave my friend alone!"

Smithy flew at the boy with the gun, swinging with his fists. The boy stepped aside and Smithy flailed past. He crashed into a bin, flapped his arms for a few panicky seconds, then toppled head-first inside.

"Misjudged that again," Smithy said, his voice echoing. "Should've thought it through. Um... Could someone...?"

The girl caught Smithy by the belt of his trousers and pulled him free. "Thanks," he said, dusting himself down, then he jumped in front of Denzel, hands raised in a karate-chop pose. "Now, stay back! I'm warning you."

The boy lowered his rifle and Smithy gave a satisfied nod. "Yeah. That's right. Back off, man. These hands are lethal in the right ... hands." He winced. "That was awkwardly phrased, but you get the idea."

The trash-ball shuddered, making Denzel and Smithy both yelp and leap back. The girl knelt beside it. She mumbled below her breath as she tied what looked like very long twigs all the way around the densely packed rubbish.

"What is that?" Denzel asked.

"Willow branches," said the girl. "Blessed by three embodiments of the goddess Brigantia, granting it binding power over the dark realms."

Denzel blinked. "Uh, cool. That was nice of her," he

said. "But I meant the rubbish-thing."

"A ghost," said the boy.

"A ghost?" said Denzel. He and Smithy began to laugh, then realised the other two weren't joining in. "What? You're not serious."

"Technically, it's an ectoplasmic manifestation," said the girl, standing up. The willow branches were tied tightly around the trash-ball, which now showed no interest in moving.

"Ah, right," said Denzel. "One of them."

The boy looked him up and down. "So … what do we do with you?"

The girl nudged him. "The bigger question is, what are we going to do with *them*."

She gestured to the school. Virtually the entire roll of pupils had gathered at the windows and doors to watch what was going on.

The boy clicked his tongue against the roof of his mouth. "The barrier's in place, right?"

The girl reached a hand past Denzel's head and extended a finger. A crackle of energy passed along her arm. "Yep."

"Then gas them," said the boy. He reached into a pocket on his belt and pulled out a piece of transparent plastic. He slipped it over his nose and mouth, then nodded at the girl to do the same. "Gas them all."

It took a few seconds for the boy's words to filter all the way through into Denzel's brain. The girl was slipping on her own mask when he finally reacted.

"What? What do you mean, 'gas them'?" he demanded, then he struggled and squirmed as the boy wrapped an arm around his chest from behind. A plastic mask was forced over the bottom half of Denzel's face.

The girl took a pouch from the gold-coloured length of rope she had tied around her waist like a belt. She tipped a handful of glittery dust into her hand. "What about him?" she said, nodding towards Smithy, who was hopping from foot to foot and swishing his hands, karate-style.

The boy shrugged. "What about him?" he said.

"Harsh," said the girl, then she pressed the dust against the invisible wall. The barrier shimmered, revealing itself as an enormous dome that covered the entire school.

"Wh-what are you doing?" Denzel demanded, but before anyone could answer, everything inside the dome was lost in a choking cloud of glittering orange.

CHAPTER 5

Denzel lifted a foot and brought his heel stamping down on the toe of the boy behind him. The boy didn't flinch.

"Steel toe caps," he growled in Denzel's ear. "But I wouldn't try anything like that again."

He released his grip and Denzel almost toppled forwards into the fog. It was all around him, swirling and sparkling like a snow globe's insides. He could just barely make out the outline of the school and imagined that he could, if he tried hard enough, just hear the screams of his classmates.

"What have you done?" he cried. "You've killed them! You've..."

SPECTRE COLLECTORS

A shimmering ripple passed all the way through the fog, and it instantly vanished. The gathered pupils gazed blankly back at Denzel.

"...Done absolutely nothing," he finished. The pupils all blinked, as if waking from a dream. One by one, they wandered off, chatting and laughing, and stuffing their faces with assorted pack lunches.

Smithy wandered over, his hands in his pockets. "All right?"

Denzel gasped with relief and threw his arms around his friend, hugging him tightly. "You're OK!"

"Get off," said Smithy, blushing slightly. "Of course I'm OK. Why wouldn't I be?"

"He won't remember anything," said the girl, joining them.

"Yes, I do," said Smithy.

"That gas you saw is actually an airborne variant of an enchanted powder we use to induce a form of amnesia. No one in the school will remember anything of what just happened."

"I remember," said Smithy.

"We've wiped it completely from their minds," said the girl. "Their psyches will fill in the blanks and come up with an explanation as to what they've been doing for the past ten minutes."

"But as for what really happened," added the boy. "No one but us three will know."

"Us four," said Smithy.

"What are you talking about?" said the girl, twitching slightly with irritation. "Your short-term memory has been wiped clean. You don't remember a thing."

"Yes, I do." Smithy pointed to the bound ball of trash. "That was a big rubbish-monster. I fell in the bin. Twice. You pulled me out, then I nearly went kung fu on you both, but, luckily for you, I chose not to."

The boy and the girl glanced at each other, neither one able to hide their shock. "What?" the girl spluttered. "But... How? How do you remember?"

Smithy tapped the side of his head. "You know what they say. An elephant never forgets."

There was a moment of silence. Denzel gently cleared his throat. "Yeah. But you're not an elephant, though, are you?"

Smithy frowned. "So?"

"So the saying doesn't apply."

It took Smithy a few moments to process this. "Wait, that saying doesn't *literally* refer to elephants, does it?"

Denzel nodded. "Yeah."

"It *literally* means *literal* elephants?"

"Of course it does," said Denzel. "What did you think

it meant?"

"Just that, you know, *no one* ever forgets," said Smithy.

Denzel shook his head. "It doesn't mean that. It means elephants."

The girl pushed between them. "Look, can we not worry about elephants right now?" She spun to face Smithy. "How were you not affected? How can you still remember?"

"Dunno." Smithy shrugged. "At a guess," he said, drawing the words out, "it's my sinuses. I have these like, what I can only describe as mucus plugs in my nose. These thick sort of chunky mucusy blobs that—"

"OK, OK, I get it," said the girl, looking somewhat queasy.

"They're like sort of snot corks, if you can imagine such a thing, that mean I can't breathe through my nose or smell anything at all. Look."

He lifted his arm and had a deep sniff of his armpit. "See? Can't smell a thing," he said. His nostrils flared. "Well, I can smell *something*, but it's *very* faint."

He tapped himself on the nose and grinned. "Mucus plugs. Don't leave home without them!"

"Great," said the girl, throwing up her arms. "He remembers. So, what do we do now?"

"We bring them in," said the boy.

"What, both of them?"

The boy looked from Denzel to Smithy and back again. He narrowed his eyes and tightened his grip on his assault rifle. "Yeah," he said. "Both of them."

Denzel and Smithy sat huddled together in the back of a white Transit van, which had now been clattering along for several minutes. They were sitting on a stainless steel box that ran down one whole side of the van's storage area and was about as far from comfortable as it was possible to get. A wooden chest had been pushed against the wall opposite. Images of demons and cryptic symbols were carved into the dark wood.

As the van rounded a corner, Smithy put his feet on the chest and leaned back, crossing his arms behind his head.

"This is the life, eh?"

Denzel stared at him. "What are you talking about?" he said, whispering so the boy and girl up front wouldn't hear. "We've been kidnapped."

Smithy's face went pale. "What? When?"

"Now!" Denzel said. He gestured frantically around the van. "What do you think this is?"

Smithy glanced around, his eyes widening. "Oh, great. Now you tell me."

Denzel had to struggle to keep his voice down. "He had a gun on us. He shoved us in here and said, 'No funny stuff or I'll shoot you.' Remember? Any of that ringing a bell?"

Smithy gulped. "I thought that was just, like, a phrase. Like 'elephants never forget'."

Denzel rammed his fist in his mouth to stop himself shouting. "A phrase?" he squeaked. "You thought 'no funny stuff or I'll shoot you' was *a phrase*?"

"What I want to know is, how is he allowed to drive?" Smithy asked. "He looks about nine!"

"No, he doesn't."

"OK, no, obviously he doesn't look nine, he's massive. But he doesn't look old enough to have a driving licence."

"He doesn't look old enough to have a gun licence, either," Denzel pointed out. "But that's not stopping him."

"Everything all right back there?" asked the girl, turning to lean over the back of her seat.

"Fine," said Denzel, but it came out squeaky, so he cleared his throat and tried again. "Fine," he said, much lower this time. Too low, if anything.

The girl smiled. It was, Denzel couldn't help but notice, quite a nice smile. "You've probably got loads of questions."

Smithy pointed at the boy. "Is he going to shoot us?"

"No," said the girl.

"Yes," said the boy.

"Maybe," the girl admitted. "He does enjoy shooting things, but as long as you don't give him any reason to shoot you, he won't."

The boy angled the rear-view mirror so Denzel and Smithy could see his eyes. "But I might," he added, glaring at them.

Denzel and Smithy exchanged a worried glance. "Maybe you should just keep quiet for a while," Denzel whispered. Smithy nodded, gave a thumbs-up, then mimed buttoning his mouth shut.

"Who are you?" Denzel asked.

"Actually, we've already met," said the girl. "At your house, yesterday."

Denzel frowned. "No, we haven't, I'd... Wait. The glittery gas stuff?"

The girl nodded. "Well, in powder form, but yes. Sorry." She held out a hand and Denzel shook it. "Samara. This is Boyle."

"*Lance Corporal* Boyle," he said, and even his voice seemed to snap to attention.

Smithy let out a sharp laugh. "Lance. Boyle," he said, grinning. "There's got to be a joke there somewhere. You know, about lancing boils."

"There is," said Boyle. "But if you make it, I swear I will shoot you in the face."

Smithy buttoned his mouth shut again, then nodded his understanding.

"I'm Denzel," said Denzel. "This is Smithy."

"Pleased to meet you properly," said Samara, flashing the smile that was definitely starting to grow on Denzel now.

He pushed the thought away. "Um… OK. But who actually are you?" He looked down at the carefully bound ball of litter that was wedged between the wooden chest and the back of the van's seats. "And what was that thing?"

"We're part of a top-secret organisation dedicated to protecting the human race from supernatural threats," said the girl. "We go by many names. The Cult of Sh'grath. The Messengers of the Allwhere. The Seventh Army of the Enlightened. Personally, though, we prefer the Spectre Collectors."

Denzel's frown deepened to the point he could see his own eyebrows. "The Spectre Collectors? So… What? You—"

"Catch ghosts. Yes," said Boyle. "The clue's right there in the name."

There was a *thud* as Smithy fell over. He immediately sat upright, his eyes wide open in shock. "You catch *ghosts*?"

"That's right," said Samara.

"*You* catch *ghosts*?" said Smithy again. "I mean... Since when? How long has this been going on?"

"Centuries," said Samara.

Smithy tick-tocked his head left to right, studying Samara and Boyle. "How old are you, exactly?"

"Well, obviously *we* haven't been doing it for centuries," Boyle snapped. "The organisation has existed for centuries."

Smithy's mouth flapped open and closed like a fish. "Well... I mean... Why have I never been informed about this?"

Denzel frowned. "Why would you have been?"

Smithy raised a finger and took a breath, as if about to speak, then changed his mind. "No, fair point. Well made," he said.

He was just getting to his feet when Boyle braked sharply. "Wah!" Smithy yelped, as he was thrown against the back of the seats. He bounced off and hit the floor again.

"We're here," said Boyle. He gestured to Denzel and Smithy. "We should blindfold them, so they can't identify our location."

Samara gave a quick shake of her head. "I don't think we need to. It's not like they'll recognise the place."

"Hey, that's the church on Wiggins Street," said Smithy, craning his neck so he could peer through the windscreen.

Samara wilted under Boyle's glare, and quietly cleared her throat. "Totally should have blindfolded them," she admitted.

She and Boyle opened their doors and jumped out. As soon as the doors slammed shut again, Smithy turned to Denzel. "We should jump them."

"We definitely shouldn't," Denzel said.

Smithy grabbed the ball of litter. It was heavier than it looked. "I'll chuck this at Lance."

"Boyle," Denzel corrected.

"What?"

"His name's Boyle. Not Lance."

Smithy frowned. "So who's Lance then?" He shook his head. "Doesn't matter. I'll chuck this at Boyle, then karate-chop the other one in the windpipe."

"That's a terrible idea," Denzel hissed. The doors began to open.

"Get ready," Smithy whispered.

"No, don't! Don't even think about it!" Denzel

protested, but it was too late. Smithy took aim, then launched the rubbish-ball through the doors just as they opened all the way. Boyle caught the ball in one hand and tucked it under his arm.

"Thanks," he said.

Smithy smiled weakly. "You're very welcome," he said. "Excellent catch, by the way."

He and Denzel jumped down from the van and splashed, ankle-deep, in a puddle. Boyle smirked. "Watch your step."

Samara sighed. "Ignore him. He thinks he's funny."

"Come on, that was pretty funny," Boyle said. "They landed right in the puddle."

"Well, maybe if you weren't also standing in it..." Samara said. Boyle looked down at the water seeping in through the lace holes in his boots. To Denzel's amazement, Samara was floating a few centimetres above the murky puddle's surface.

Boyle muttered below his breath and backed out of the puddle. Samara closed the doors and pressed her hand against the metal. "Go with Boyle, I'll catch you up in a second," she said. "And stop looking so worried. We're the good guys."

Denzel and Smithy followed Boyle towards a narrow path that led around the back of the church. After they'd gone a few paces there was a *whoosh* from behind them. Denzel turned to see Samara striding along, swinging her arms. The van, however, was nowhere to be seen.

Smithy leaned in to Denzel. "What are they going to do with us?"

"I don't know," Denzel admitted.

"I think Samantha likes me," Smithy whispered.

"Samara," Denzel corrected.

"I think Samara likes me," said Smithy. "Watch this."

Smithy turned and walked backwards alongside Denzel. "Hey, excuse me. Miss? What's your name again?"

"Samara."

"Nothing!" cried Smithy. "What's *Samara* with you?" He broke into a broad grin. "See what I did there?"

Boyle glanced back over his shoulder. "Want me to shoot him?"

Samara shook her head. "Um... No. It's fine."

Smithy winked at her, then turned back to Denzel. "See?" he whispered.

"See what?"

"She could totally have had me shot dead there, but she didn't," Smithy pointed out. He began to sing quietly. "Smithy and Samara, sitting in a tree, K-I-S-S-I—"

"This is it," snapped Boyle, coming to a sudden halt

beside what appeared to be a perfectly normal – if ancient – wooden door. There was a fearsome-looking iron knocker fixed to the wood at head height. It had been designed to look like the face of some freaky frog-like creature with bulging eyes.

The door was tucked around the back of the church and was well hidden from the street, but Boyle still glanced around to make sure no one was watching. Once he was satisfied the coast was clear, he leaned closer to the frog-thing and stared into its eyes.

There was a faint *bleep* and the door opened a fraction, revealing nothing but darkness beyond. Boyle stepped aside and gestured into the gloom with his gun. "Women and children first," he said, eyeballing Denzel and Smithy.

Smithy sniffed indignantly. "We're not children," he said. "Or women." He glanced at Denzel. "We're not, are we?"

"Not women, but we are children, yeah."

"Oh. Right. Yes, so we are," said Smithy. He nodded to Boyle. "In that case, thanks very much," he said, then he and Denzel clutched each other by the sleeves of their school uniforms, and stepped through the doorway into the waiting dark.

CHAPTER 6

The room beyond the door was just a few paces long. Boyle and Samara stepped in after them and pulled the door closed, plunging the place even deeper into darkness.

A moment later, a light above their heads clicked on and Denzel saw several versions of himself staring back at him. They were inside a narrow, rectangular space with mirrors covering every wall. The back of the door was also mirrored, and Denzel could see himself from virtually every angle without having to move his head.

"Is this your secret base?" Smithy asked. "It's pretty small."

"I think this is probably just the lift," Denzel said. "Right?"

Samara nodded and smiled her not-unpleasant smile. She jabbed one of just two buttons mounted on the wall. "It takes a while," she said, crossing her hands behind her back as the lift began to creep downwards.

Boyle still had the trash-ball tucked under one arm. His gun was lowered by his side, but the way he was holding it suggested he was ready to snap it up again at any moment. Denzel tried smiling at him, but it only made Boyle's scowl deepen, so he stopped quite quickly.

They all stood in awkward silence. Samara whistled softly until she spotted Boyle glaring at her. The whistle faded away, then petered out completely.

"Here's one for you," said Smithy, breaking the quiet.

Denzel shook his head. "Don't," he urged.

"What would you rather have, right?" Smithy continued. "Hands where your feet are, and feet where your hands are, *or*, feet where your hands are, and hands where your feet are."

"That's the same thing," said Samara.

Smithy shook his head. "No, it isn't."

"She's right," said Denzel. "It's the same."

"*No*," Smithy protested. "So, listen. Pay attention. You can have *hands* where your *feet* are and *feet* where your *hands* are, *or* feet where… Oh yeah, it's the same thing."

He rolled his eyes slowly, as if searching for something. "OK, what about this, then. Would you rather have the hands-and-feet-swapped thing like I said, right?"

Denzel sighed. "Right."

"*Or* have a head made of onions?" Smithy folded his arms and rocked back on his heels. Boyle stared at him blankly for several long seconds, then turned to Samara.

"*Now* do you want me to shoot him?" he asked, but before she could answer, the lift bumped to a stop and the door swung sharply inwards. The piercing screams of an alarm filled the narrow space.

"On your knees! Move, move!" roared a voice, and the lift was suddenly packed full of angry people. A girl with closely cropped hair and a fiery scar running down one whole side of her face led the pack. She pointed a handgun directly at Denzel's head, and he automatically put his hands up. The gun was so large it would have been comical, were Denzel not so busy being utterly terrified.

The girl wore a uniform similar to Boyle's, and behind her were two others – a boy and another girl – dressed in the same blue and silver camouflage.

Further behind those two, Denzel was vaguely aware of some other people dressed in tunics and robes, but he was far more interested for the moment in the gun that was pointing directly between his eyes.

"You heard me! On your knees!" the girl barked.

"Don't. It's OK," Boyle told Denzel. "Relax, Knightley. They're with us."

Knightley didn't take her eyes off Denzel. One of the other soldiers had a rifle trained on Smithy, who, Denzel noticed, was already kneeling.

"Sensors picked up a level four freeform phantom in this lift," Knightley shouted. She really seemed to like shouting. "So I'm not prepared to take any chances. On your knees, boy. Now."

Denzel started to kneel, but Boyle's gun swung towards him. "Denzel, if you get on your knees I swear I will shoot you myself."

"Oh ... come on," Denzel protested, freezing halfway to the floor. His eyes flicked between the two guns, trying to decide which of the two looked like it'd do the most damage. Boyle's came out on top, but not by much.

"Does that apply to me, too?" asked Smithy. "Because I've been kneeling for a while, so it doesn't seem very fair if you shoot me now."

"Get up," Boyle said.

"Stay down," barked Knightley.

"Wow, I'm literally drowning in macho nonsense

here," said Samara. She yanked the trash-ball from under Boyle's arm and thrust it towards Knightley. "Here."

Knightley tore her eyes away from Denzel long enough to glance at the ball. "What's this?"

"A level four freeform phantom," said Samara. "We couldn't gem it, but it's all bound and ready for processing."

Knightley kept her weapon trained on Denzel, who was still frozen midway to his knees. His thighs now felt like they were on fire, and he had a nasty feeling he was about to fart.

Samara raised the trash-ball higher. Knightley lowered her head enough for her to touch her tongue against a crumpled-up paper plate. Denzel and Smithy both recoiled in disgust.

"Ew," Smithy muttered. "Lips that touch bin-monsters will never touch mine."

Knightley rolled her tongue around inside her mouth, then lowered her gun. Denzel immediately straightened up with a groan of relief. Holstering the weapon, Knightley snatched the trash-ball from Samara and crisply about-turned.

"You're welcome, Knightley," said Boyle. She hesitated, as if she were about to reply, then marched ahead, forcing the others to back hurriedly out of her path.

"Well, she seemed nice," said Denzel, letting out a breath he hadn't realised he was holding in. Boyle rounded on him.

"What did you say?" he demanded.

"Um… Just that she seemed nice," said Denzel. "But, you know, sarcastically."

"Because she didn't," Smithy added, still down on his knees. "She didn't seem nice *at all*."

"Why would she be 'nice'?" growled Boyle. "She's not here to be nice, she's here to do a job. A job that keeps people like you safe."

"OK, OK," said Denzel. "I only said it because I thought you didn't like her."

"I *don't* like her," Boyle snapped.

"No one likes her," Samara confirmed.

"Well… OK," said Denzel, floundering badly. "Good. So… I mean… That's all fine. Why are you shouting at me?"

Boyle twitched with irritation, then wheeled around to face the door. The squeals of the alarm stopped and he swung his rifle strap over his shoulder. "Come on. Let's go and see Quinn."

He stomped out of the lift. Samara turned to Denzel. "Don't worry. He's a pussycat when you get to know him. Just, you know, a really angry one. Like a tiger or a lion.

With a big gun." She smiled cheerfully. "Now, come on. Off we go."

After helping Smithy to his feet, Denzel followed Boyle out of the lift and into a brightly lit corridor. The walls were a gunmetal grey, and the floor had been polished to a mirror-like sheen. It all looked stark and clinical, aside from the enormous oil painting hung directly opposite the lift door.

"Who's that?" Smithy asked, peering up at the painting. It showed a middle-aged woman in a business suit, and would have been completely unremarkable were it not for her hands. In one hand, she held a handgun not unlike the one Denzel had recently had pointed at his face, while the other hand clutched what seemed to be a ball of blue fire.

Her mouth was smiling, but the rest of her face wasn't joining in. In fact, the longer Denzel looked at it, the less it resembled a real smile at all. It was the smile of someone who had tried to learn how to smile from a book, but had never read further than the first few chapters.

"That's Director Quinn," said Samara. "That's who we're taking you to meet."

"Cool! Will her hand be on fire?" Smithy asked.

Samara chewed her lip. "Let's hope not."

"Why is her hand on fire?" Denzel wondered.

"It's supposed to symbolise her ability with magic," said Samara. "And the gun symbolises—"

"That she likes shooting people?" Smithy guessed.

"That she's equally as comfortable with technology and science," said Samara. "She invented that gun she's holding, actually."

"Whoa," said Smithy. "Did she invent fire, too?"

Samara stared at him for a moment, but saw nothing but genuine curiosity on his face. "Uh, no. No, I don't think that was her."

"Hurry up," said Boyle. He was waiting along the corridor, where it curved off to the left. The other direction curved to the right, and Denzel got the impression that if they walked far enough one way, they'd eventually circle all the way around.

Samara gestured for the boys to follow Boyle. He marched at a ridiculous pace, and they had to half-walk, half-run to keep up. As they scurried along, they passed dozens of doors on both sides of the corridor. Each door looked more or less like all the others – same dull grey finish, same polished brass handle – with just a little plaque beside each one to tell them apart.

They were walking too quickly to read most of them, but Denzel recognised a few words as they passed, like "paranormal", and "spectral", and, on one particularly wide plaque, "transpandimensional".

"What are all these places?" he asked. He gestured to a door just ahead. The plaque read: *Spectral Storage 8*.

"That's one of our ghost vaults," Samara explained, as if it was the most normal statement in the world. "The ones in there aren't too bad. Mostly just murderers. A few flesh-eaters."

"An eyeball-harvester," said Boyle.

"Oh yes, she was a fun one," said Samara. "The really dangerous ones are kept way down below."

"Oh. Right," Denzel squeaked, wishing he'd never asked.

"So, that alarm thing?" said Smithy. "It detects any ghosts that come in here?"

"It does," Samara confirmed.

"Like, *all* ghosts?" Smithy asked. "Like, could ghosts get in here without you knowing about it?"

Boyle snorted. "No."

"Right. Good," said Smithy. "Interesting."

"So how come all this is here?" asked Denzel. "And not in London or somewhere?"

"Why would we be in London?" asked Boyle.

"Isn't that where all the, like, government stuff is?"

Boyle glanced back. "We're not part of the government."

"It's all to do with spectral density," Samara said.

"I knew it!" said Smithy. "I was totally going to say that. Spectrum destiny."

"Spectral density," Samara corrected.

Smithy nodded and smiled. "Yep, that's the one. Carry on."

"Basically, dotted around the world are a number of ghost hotspots. Places where the ghosts and spirits gather in greater than average numbers. There are Spectre Collector branches at most of them."

"Why?" asked Denzel.

"Why what?"

"Why do they gather in those places?"

They stopped outside a set of imposing wooden doors that blocked the corridor ahead of them. "We don't know," Samara admitted. "We just know we're here because that's where the ghosts are." She fidgeted with her robe and adjusted the rings on her fingers. Boyle raised a hand to the door and hesitated, knuckles poised.

"One moment," said a voice from inside before Boyle could knock.

They waited outside the door, Boyle standing to attention, the rest of them in various states of slouching. "Did you want to phone your parents or anything?" asked Samara in a hushed voice. "Give them some excuse in case you're late?"

"They won't be home yet," Denzel said.

Samara turned to Smithy. "You?"

"Me? What?" Smithy said. "I wasn't listening."

"She was asking if you wanted to phone your mum and dad," Denzel said. He hoped he hadn't put his foot in it – Smithy had never spoken about his parents before, and Denzel realised he had no idea what his home life was like.

"Nah, they won't be around just now," Smithy said.

"Come," ordered the voice from beyond the door.

Boyle glanced briefly at Samara, then took hold of both brass door handles. The handles lit up for a fraction of a second, then gave a reassuring *bleep*. Both doors swung inwards all on their own, and Denzel was presented with a view of the most lavish office he'd ever seen.

His parents had an office at home, but it was a broom cupboard compared to this one. Denzel could have kicked a football in here and there was a good chance it wouldn't reach the other door at the opposite end of the room.

The wood-panelled walls swept around in swooshing curves. On one side they were lined with bookcases, while the curves opposite were plastered with impossibly thin computer screens, all displaying reams of numbers and symbols.

The bare floorboards had been varnished to such a brilliant sheen it was almost a shame they were mostly hidden beneath a red-and-gold-patterned rug. The rug looked big enough to carpet every room in Denzel's house, with enough left over to make a good dent in the garden.

High above the floor hung an antique chandelier. At least, Denzel assumed it was an antique. It was a big heavy thing and looked absolutely ancient, with lots of swooping metal curves and dangling bit of glass. The bulbs nestled in it seemed to be powered by electricity, though, so maybe it wasn't as old as it looked.

Slap bang in the middle of the room, at the centre of a horseshoe-shaped desk, sat the woman from the portrait. Her hair was a little more grey, but even without the gun and the handful of fire, Denzel had no problem recognising her. It was the not-really-smile that gave her away. The not-really-smile that was currently pointed squarely in Denzel's direction.

Boyle stepped through the door, snapped to attention, and fired off a sharp salute. "At ease, lance corporal," the woman said. Her voice had the same false lightness as her expression, and Denzel had to fight the urge to back away. "Come in. Close the door," she instructed. "Let me get a closer look at you."

Samara half-shoved Denzel and Smithy into the room, then pulled the doors closed behind her. "Sorry to interrupt, Director Quinn," she began. "We thought you should meet this..."

Quinn made a dismissive gesture with a hand, then crooked one of her fingers at Denzel, beckoning him closer. He shot Samara a glance and she gave him an encouraging nod.

Slowly, and completely against his better judgement, Denzel approached the desk. Sitting there in the middle of it, Quinn reminded Denzel of a spider at the centre of a web. He tried not to think too much about that as she beckoned him closer still.

"So, you're the boy who was attacked twice in two days," she said, once he was close enough to touch the desk.

"Uh, yeah," said Denzel. "I mean, apparently."

"And I hear you can see poltergeists," said the director. "Do you know why that's interesting?"

Denzel shook his head. "Because no one can see poltergeists, Denzel," Quinn continued. She leaned forwards, placing her elbows on the mahogany desktop and steepling her fingers in front of her. That almost-smile was still fixed in place. "Which means either you're someone very special indeed, the likes of whom we've never met before … or you're a liar."

She slammed both hands down on the desk. Denzel jumped and let out an involuntary yelp of fright, and, for just a fleeting moment, Quinn's smile was real.

"And I fully intend to find out which."

CHAPTER 7

Denzel stood in a room roughly the size of his school gym hall. Three Transit van-sized metal containers were lined up in front of him, each one perched on the prongs of a different forklift truck. There was a window in the end of each box, through which Denzel could see that two of them were empty. The third, however, was not.

"That one," he said, pointing to the middle container.

Director Quinn stood beside him, her arms folded. She was turned side-on to the containers, so she could watch Denzel's face up close. "Are you sure?" she asked.

Denzel nodded. Inside the container, tucked into the shadows near the back, he could see a shape made of what looked to be black smoke. It had long, trembling tentacles that it had wrapped around itself like a cocoon.

On Denzel's "Most Mind-Blowingly Terrifying Things Ever" scale – which he had only very recently had any reason to invent – it was just a notch below the trash-monster. And yet, as he watched the thing, he couldn't help but feel a pang of sympathy for it.

"It's that one. It's the middle one," he said, pointing again.

Boyle stepped past him and aimed his rifle at the middle container. Almost immediately, a red light near the base of the barrel began to blink. Boyle turned to Quinn and gave one quick nod.

"Interesting," said the director. "What does it look like?"

"Sort of black and smoky," Denzel said. He took another step closer to the glass. "And ... frightened. I think it's scared."

"Oh heavens, no. I don't think so, Denzel," said Quinn. "It can't be scared. Poltergeists don't get scared. They're animals."

Denzel turned. "I'm pretty sure animals get scared."

"I know ducks definitely do," Smithy volunteered.

"Exactly," Denzel began, then he frowned and glanced at his friend. "How do you know that?"

68

Smithy's lips went thin. "It's a long story," he said. "You don't want to know."

"It's a spectre. A ghost. Trust me, it's no more capable of emotion than the box containing it is capable of dancing the fandango," Quinn said. Denzel peered through the glass. The shape was vibrating now, and although he couldn't hear anything, he would have sworn he could *feel* it whimpering somewhere inside his head.

Boyle put two fingers in his mouth and let out a shrill whistle. One by one, the forklifts started to reverse. "What'll you do with it?" Denzel asked, watching the box retreat.

"It'll go to Spectral Storage to be stored," Samara said. "Don't worry, nothing's going to happen to it."

"Apart from being 'stored', you mean?" Denzel said.

There was a loud shout from a driver as one of the other reversing forklifts clipped the back wheel of the middle one. Both vehicles rocked sideways in opposite directions, and the poltergeist saw its chance. It shot from one side of the container to the other, slamming itself hard against the wall. Already unbalanced, the box rolled off the forklift's prongs and hit the ground with a deafening *clang*. The sound echoed around the room like the peal of an old church bell.

The glass pane in the window splintered. It wasn't

much – barely a hairline split – but black smoke quickly began to seep through the crack. "Um... Um..." Denzel stammered, pointing to where the smoke was already forming into long dark tentacles. "The thing. The thing's getting out."

Boyle raised his weapon. "Where?"

"The window!" yelped Denzel. There was a flash of blinding white and a crash of shattering glass as Boyle opened fire. Denzel blinked rapidly, trying to clear away the dazzling white spots that were now floating in front of his eyes.

"Did you get it?" Quinn demanded.

Boyle spun on the spot, sweeping with his rifle. "Negative."

Denzel's vision returned in time for him to see the smoky shape hurtling towards him, its six black tentacles snapping like whips in the air. He stumbled back, knocking Smithy aside, his mouth flapping open and closed in panic as he jabbed a finger towards the approaching apparition.

"There!"

Boyle's finger tightened on the trigger. The weapon's barrel glowed white. The poltergeist lunged. Just before it was swallowed by the blinding light, Denzel saw the thing's tentacles twist into familiar shapes.

No, not shapes. More than shapes. Letters. Six shadowy letters silhouetted against the light, forming two words.

Help us.

The light faded and the shape was gone, but the words were still there, imprinted on Denzel's retinas. He lay sprawled on the floor, breathing heavily and trying to figure out what had just happened.

"That's quite the talent you have," said Quinn, stepping over him. She held out a hand and, after a moment's hesitation, Denzel took it. Her grip was surprisingly strong. She hoisted Denzel to his feet, then hit him with that not-quite-smile. "You would be a valuable addition to the Cult of Sh'grath."

"What?" spluttered Boyle, but a single look from Quinn silenced him.

"To the who?" Denzel asked.

"Us," said Samara. She took the red gemstone Boyle handed to her, and began wrapping it in willow branches. "She means you'd be a great addition to the Spectre Collectors."

Smithy leaned in and grinned. "You mean *we'd* be a great addition to the Spectre Collectors," he said.

Quinn looked Smithy up and down, as if noticing him for the first time and not particularly approving of what she saw. "Who is this … *person*?"

"He's Smithy," said Denzel. "He's my friend."

"We had to bring him in," said Samara. "The wipe didn't work."

"I've got mucus plugs," said Smithy, pointing to the bridge of his nose.

"Well," breathed Quinn. "You must be very proud."

She turned her attention back to Denzel. "As I was saying, *you* would be a very valuable asset to us here. You have a most unusual talent. We could use you in the field. You could make a real difference to the world, Denzel. A real difference."

She fixed him with her not-smile, and Denzel was suddenly very aware that everyone else was watching him, too. He fiddled with his hands and cleared his throat. "No," he said. "I mean, thanks. I mean, *no thanks*."

Quinn's expression didn't change. "Oh. I see," she said. Then she glanced at the others. "Leave us."

Boyle and Samara both caught Smithy under an arm and carried him towards the door. "Hey, what are you doing? Get off!" Smithy protested, bicycling his legs in the air.

"Relax. She's just going to talk to him. He's going to be fine," said Samara. They stepped through the door. "We're the good guys, remember?" Samara assured him, and the door swung closed with a *clang*.

The moment the door closed, Quinn relaxed. She smiled at Denzel, and this time there was a flicker of actual warmth in there somewhere.

"I know all this must be hard to take in. Ghosts. Secret societies. Flying sheep."

"Sheep?" said Denzel.

Quinn's eyes widened. "Oh, no. That wasn't you, was it? Forget I mentioned it. The point is, I couldn't believe any of it when I was first brought in, either," she said. She gazed past Denzel into the middle distance. "That was a long time ago. A long time."

She gave herself a shake and turned back to him. "My father was part of the organisation at the time, of course. His mother before him, her father before her, as is tradition. That's how it works. Membership, and all it entails, is passed down through the generations."

"So ... Samara and Boyle?"

"Their parents were Spectre Collectors, yes. Father, in Samara's case, mother in Boyle's. Just like they were, I was introduced to it all from a young age, but even though I'd been prepared..." She put her hands beside her head and mimed her head exploding. "It was mind-blowing stuff."

The forklift that the box had fallen off was parked just

a few metres away. Quinn strolled over to it and hopped up so she was sitting on one of the prongs. She nodded towards the one next to her, and Denzel clambered up to take a seat.

"I was four years old when they first told me everything," Quinn continued. "They ... *we* recruit young because children and teenagers are better equipped to see beyond the normal and into the paranormal. Although, you take it to something of a new extreme, I must say."

Quinn gazed down at her polished brogue shoes and swung her legs back and forth. She looked strange there, this middle-aged woman in a business suit, perched on a forklift, idly swinging her legs. For a moment, Denzel could almost imagine her as that four-year-old, but then she spoke again and the moment passed.

"I told my dad no at first. Ran away, actually. Couldn't face the truth of what was out there, or the responsibility of having to help do something about it."

"Why did you come back?" Denzel asked.

Quinn laughed. "Because I was four. I barely made it to the end of the street." She gazed past him, into the distance. "And, I suppose, because I knew I *could* do something about it," Quinn said, fixing Denzel with a look so sincere he felt tears spring to the corners of his eyes. "Even then, I knew I could stop people being scared, or hurt, or even killed by those ... abominations. Look at you, for example."

"Me?"

Quinn nodded. "Twice in forty-eight hours, you've been attacked by malevolent spirits. If it weren't for our operatives – my operatives – there's no saying what might have happened to you. They saved you, and now you have an opportunity to save others."

Denzel smiled weakly, but said nothing.

"It may not even be for long. Between you and me, I'm working on something that – I hope – will render us obsolete," Quinn said. "Something that will rid the world of the supernatural threats it faces, once and for all. But until then, we are still needed. And we could use your help."

She hopped down from the prong and took Denzel's hands in hers. "Join us, Denzel," she said, staring deep into his eyes. "Make a difference. To the world. To yourself."

Denzel hesitated. "I don't know, I mean... It's all a bit, you know? Mad."

Quinn laughed again. "It is. You're right. That's exactly what I said when I first found out about it all. Or after I'd stopped sobbing uncontrollably, at least. It's unbelievable. All of it. But it's real. Give us a try, Denzel. One day. Give us twenty-four hours," she said. "Then, if it's not for you, you can go home."

"What about my dads? What will I tell them?" Denzel asked.

"I'll take care of it. I've been covering up the truth for four decades – I'm sure I can come up with an explanation that will satisfy your parents for one night."

Denzel nodded. "Twenty-four hours?" he said. "Then I can go?"

"You can go now, if you like; you're not a prisoner here," Quinn said. "But I'd love you to try us out. Just for a day."

"What about Smithy?"

Quinn seemed confused by the question. "What about him?"

"Does he get to stay, too?"

"I'm afraid not," Quinn said, sounding genuinely sorry. "I'm already breaking several rules inviting you in. Bringing your friend in, too, is out of the question."

She placed a hand on his shoulder. Her fingers gripped him firmly, and he got the impression he couldn't pull away, even if he tried. "So, Denzel," she asked, her eyes boring deep into his. "What's it to be?"

CHAPTER 8

Smithy shifted his weight from foot to foot as they waited for the lift. He glanced over Denzel's shoulder, to where Boyle and Samara stood waiting.

"I don't think you should stay here, Denzel," Smithy whispered. "You sure about this?"

"Not really," Denzel admitted. He shrugged. "But, I dunno. It might be important. And it's only one day."

"And one night," Smithy pointed out. "In an underground bunker filled with ghosts and crazy gun-people."

"I'm sure it'll be fine," Denzel said. "I mean, what's the worst that could happen?"

"You could be torn apart by ghost wolves," said Smithy. "That would be pretty bad."

"Right, but—"

"Or attacked by a creepy little girl ghost with a clown doll that just laughs and goes 'mama, mama, mama' over and over again, and, like, you can hear her coming, but you can't see her until she's right there in front of your face, and by then it's too late to—"

"Right, yes, I get it!" said Denzel. "That probably is the worst thing that could happen, but I don't think it will."

"Oh," said Smithy, looking a little disappointed. "Be cool if it did though, wouldn't it?"

The lift door swung open behind Smithy. Denzel smiled. "Yeah, it'd be pretty cool. I'll see you tomorrow, OK?"

With a final glance at Boyle and Samara, Smithy stepped into the lift. "Yeah. See you tomorrow," he said, then the door closed and Denzel listened to the rumbling of the machinery as Smithy was carried back up towards the surface.

He turned, suddenly feeling more alone than he'd ever felt, and tried his best to smile. "Right, then," he said. "Where do we start?"

Denzel stood facing Samara near the centre of a chalk

circle. He had no idea how big the room they were in was, as the light from the five candles positioned around the circle's edge only extended a couple of metres into the gloom. Beyond that was darkness, and somewhere in the dark was the door they'd entered through.

"Before we begin, let me quickly explain about how it all works," Samara said.

"How magic works?"

"How the organisation works. I can't 'quickly explain' how magic works. That takes years."

"Gotcha," said Denzel. "Should I write anything down?"

Samara shrugged. "If you want."

"I don't have a pen or anything," Denzel said.

Samara tutted. "Well don't write it down, then." She cleared her throat. "Basically, there are two divisions. Oberon – which I'm in. We focus on the magical arts. And Vulteron. They're more interested in science, technology and guns. And blowing stuff up."

"Like Boyle," said Denzel.

"Exactly. Like Boyle. An Oberon and a Vulteron are always partnered together, the idea being we complement each other. Things we can do, they can't, and vice versa. That's the theory, at least."

"Got it," said Denzel. "So what one am I going to be?"

"That's what we're here to find out," said Samara. "Together, Oberons and Vulterons investigate paranormal disturbances. Ghosts, demons, dark magic – that sort of stuff."

"Gotcha," said Denzel. "Why?"

"Why what?" asked Samara.

"Why do you investigate all that stuff?"

Samara frowned, like the question had never occurred to her. "Well, I mean, because if we didn't they'd kill everyone and end the world."

"Oh. Right. Fair enough," said Denzel. "Good job you're on the case, then."

"Exactly," said Samara. She glanced around into the shadows. "So … what did you think of Director Quinn?"

"She seems… I don't know," said Denzel. "I thought she was going to be horrible, but she was pretty nice, in the end. She's really been doing this since she was four, though?"

"Yeah," said Samara. "We all get recruited young, but never that young."

"Must've been hard on her," said Denzel.

Samara opened her mouth as if about to say something, then thought better of it. "Yeah. Must have been," she said. "Now, let's get to work." She held a hand out to him, fist clenched. "Here."

Denzel fist-bumped her and smiled. "Right back at you."

"No. I meant take this," she said, turning her hand over and opening it. A chunky grey metal ring sat in the centre of her palm. It was roughly the size and shape of a sovereign ring, with a cryptic red symbol painted on the top.

Denzel took the ring and rolled it around in his hand. Samara watched him with interest. "Feel anything?"

"Uh… It's heavier than it looks," said Denzel.

"What about the temperature? Does it feel cold, hot…?"

Denzel squeezed the ring in his hand for a moment. "Not really."

"Not warm, even…?"

Denzel shook his head. "Nope."

Samara tried to hide her disappointment, but didn't make a very good job of it. "No, that's fine. That's totally fine. Put it on. Middle finger, right hand."

Denzel slipped the ring on and spent a few seconds adjusting to the feeling of it. He'd never worn jewellery before, and even if he had, this ugly hunk of scratched metal wouldn't have been his first choice.

"That's a Feurety Ring," Samara said. "Do you know who Feurety is?"

Denzel snorted. "Do I know who Feurety is? Do *I know* who Feurety is?" He laughed. "I can't believe you're asking me that."

"You don't, do you?"

Denzel shook his head. "No," he admitted. "Not a clue."

"He's an ancient demon who some people worship as the god of fire," Samara explained.

"You mean wor*shipped*, right?" said Denzel.

Samara shook her head. "I mean worship. Present tense." She pointed at Denzel's hand. "Feurety Rings help Oberons create and control fire."

Denzel shot the ring a wary glance. "That sounds … risky."

"It is," Samara agreed. "But it's still just a parlour trick compared to the bigger stuff, and I thought it better you burn your eyebrows off than accidentally punch a hole into the Spectral Realm."

"Why, what would that do?" Denzel asked.

Samara stepped up beside him. "Nothing good." She held a hand out in front of her, fist clenched. "Copy me."

Denzel did as he was told. "Good," said Samara, and Denzel felt a little flutter of pride at his ability to correctly put his arm out in front of him. "Now, when I say to, I want you to both say and think a word at the same time."

"Any word?" asked Denzel.

"No, of course not any word! One specific word, which I'll tell you in a minute," Samara said. "But you can't just say it, you have to fill your head with it. Push out every other thought until that word is the only thing in the world. Can you do that?"

"Probably not," Denzel admitted. "But I'll give it a go."

"OK. The word is Flereous," said Samara. "Got it?"

Denzel nodded. "I think so."

Samara stepped back. "Go for it."

Denzel took a deep breath. He held out a hand. He smiled awkwardly. "Sorry, what was it again?"

"Flereous," said Samara.

Denzel nodded. "Right, got it," he said. "Totally got it. Here goes." He took another deep breath. "Flereous."

Nothing happened.

"It's OK," said Samara. "You won't get it first time."

"Flereous," said Denzel again. "Flereous, Flereous, Flereous!"

"Or the first five times, necessarily," said Samara. "Are you thinking it?"

"Yes," said Denzel.

"Well, clearly you're not."

"I am!" Denzel insisted. He felt himself start to blush, so he gritted his teeth and thrust his fist towards the empty space ahead of him. "Flereous. Flereous! Fle-re-ous! Argh! It's pointless. He gave his hand a shake. "Is this thing even on? You've given me a dud ring. It isn't working."

"Flereous," said Samara. Denzel yelped in shock as a billowing jet of flame erupted from the symbol on the ring and almost scorched his face. He turned, panicked, sweeping the crackling flame around in a half-circle.

The flames licked up the outside of Samara's robe, and the material ignited around her feet. Hissing in fright, she raised a hand and muttered something in a language Denzel didn't understand. The flames spluttered and died away. As the crackling of the fire faded, the only sound in the room was a faint whimpering from Denzel, who stared at the ring in disbelief.

"OK, introduction to magic over," Samara said, gazing sadly at the charcoaled hem of her robe. "I think it's time to hand you over to Boyle."

CHAPTER 9

Denzel stood in a warehouse-like room, staring up at a construction of metal and glass that loomed over him. He was bending backwards to the point he was sure he was going to cause himself damage, but even from that angle it wasn't easy to see the top of the object before him.

"What did you say it was, again?" Denzel asked.

"It's the K-11 Alpha 9 spectral combat armour," Boyle said. "More commonly referred to as the Spook Suit."

"Right," said Denzel, stepping back so he could more comfortably see the thing. It was vaguely person-shaped. At least, it would have been, if people were roughly the height of a double-decker bus. It had two massive arms, four enormous legs, and a body so huge none of the rest of it looked even slightly out of proportion.

The Spook Suit's head was a sleek curve of glass and chrome, and while the whole thing looked like a serious piece of kit, Denzel couldn't help but think it would've made the perfect villain in an episode of *Power Rangers*.

"So ... what does it do?" Denzel asked.

Boyle let out a single "Ha!" without any hint of amusement whatsoever. "What *doesn't* it do?"

He clapped his gloved hands together twice, then parted them carefully. A floating 3D image of the Spook Suit appeared in the air between his palms. Denzel stepped closer and stared at it in wonder.

"Cool!"

"I know, right?" said Boyle, doing something with his face that came within spitting distance of being a smile. "Holographic projection locked on to sensors in the gloves. Watch this."

He reached out and carefully took hold of the hologram's right arm, then raised it out to the side. The Spook Suit let out a loud hydraulic hiss, making Denzel jump back in fright. A moment later, the suit's arm rose to match the position of the hologram's.

"Pretty cool, huh?" said Boyle.

Denzel nodded. "Amazing. Can I try?"

Boyle held up his gloved hands. "Not without these. Now, pay attention," he said, moving his hands in a series of elaborate gestures. "I'm going to demonstrate its offensive capabilities."

There was a *whirr* from within the suit, and two guns swivelled into position, one on each shoulder. No, not guns. Guns didn't do them justice. These things were cannons. Each one had a slightly different design, but neither looked like something you'd want to be at the wrong end of.

"Guided weapon systems with interchangeable ammunition, offering six and eight types of rounds respectively," Boyle said. He pointed at the gun on the left. "This one here's got all your traditional types. Incendiary, high explosive, stun, rapid-fire, that sort of thing. You know, the classics."

"Classics. Definitely," said Denzel. He nodded, despite already having forgotten most of what Boyle had just said. "What about the other one?"

"Those are more specialised. The other stuff, that's available anywhere. That's basic warfare ammunition, but the gun on the right there? That one's just for us."

"So ... what?" said Denzel. "It lets you shoot ghosts?"

Boyle snorted. "No. We use guns to shoot ghosts.

With the Spook Suit, we shoot *gods*."

Denzel blinked. He jammed his little finger in his ear and wriggled it back and forth, then pulled it out with a *pop*. "Sorry, I must have misheard," he said. "For a minute there I thought you said you used it to shoot gods."

"You heard right," said Boyle. "Well, technically they're demons, but same thing, mostly."

"Same thing?" said Denzel.

"Mostly," said Boyle. "We don't only deal with ghosts, we deal with any supernatural threats, however large. Sometimes that requires some pretty major firepower."

Denzel looked around. There were several metal shelves all containing locked cases. "What else do you have? Are these other weapons?"

He picked up one of the boxes, then jumped as Boyle yelled, "Don't touch that!"

Denzel dropped the box back on the shelf and backed away. "Why, what is it?"

"It's a Spectral Disruptor. It breaks down supernatural energy. It's dangerous."

"What, more dangerous than the giant killer robot?" Denzel asked.

"Potentially, yes," said Boyle. "And it's not a robot. Like I said, it's combat armour."

"Whoa," said Denzel, looking the suit up and down

again. "Someone wears that thing?"

Boyle sighed. "Were you listening to anything I said?"

"Bits of it," Denzel admitted.

"The suit can be worn, or it can be operated remotely with the gloves," Boyle explained. He pointed to a set of heavy iron doors at the back of the room. "But the Spook Suit's just a toy compared to what's in there."

Denzel followed his gaze. "Ooh. What's in there?"

"That's the Advanced Weapons Vault. It's where we keep the time bomb," said Boyle in a slightly breathless whisper.

Denzel frowned. "What, one of those ones with the alarm clock and the dynamite, like they use in cartoons?"

"No," said Boyle. "A *time* bomb. It's called the Quantum Nullifier. It's a bomb designed to break time itself."

"I have no idea what that even means," Denzel admitted.

"No one does," said Boyle. "Not in any detail, anyway. No one really knows where it came from, or who built it. By the markings on it, it predates the Spectre Collectors by a couple of hundred years. It's a bit of a mystery, but our best guess is that if that bomb triggers, it'll literally unravel the fabric of time."

Denzel scratched his head. "Yeah, but ... what does that actually involve? Everything starts happening at the same time? Nothing happens ever? What happens if you blow up time?"

Boyle shrugged. "I don't know. Like I say, no one does. But let's hope we never find out."

He turned to find Denzel staring at the gloves. "So … the robot suit," Denzel began.

"Spook Suit," corrected Boyle. "What about it?"

"Can I have a go?"

Boyle shook his head.

"Come on," Denzel urged. "I'm supposed to be learning things, right?"

"Yes, but you don't start with the dangerous stuff," Boyle said.

"I started with magic," said Denzel. "That's pretty dangerous."

Boyle snorted. "Yeah, right. Not as dangerous as this."

"I dunno…" said Denzel. "Samara seemed to think it was way more dangerous than your stuff. And cooler. She gave me a ring that shoots fire."

"She did, did she? Fine," said Boyle, yanking off the gloves. "If you think magic's impressive, try these."

Denzel's eyes lit up. He fumbled his way into the gloves. "Great!" he cheered. He flexed his fingers and clapped his hands together. The gloves let out a series of soft *bleeps*. "So, now what do—"

SPECTRE COLLECTORS

Behind him, two rocket boosters ignited on the Spook Suit's feet, firing it upwards at tremendous speed. It smashed against the roof, zipped left and right like a deflating balloon, then fell to the ground with a *crash* that seemed to shake the whole complex.

Denzel looked over at the fallen armour. He looked at Boyle's narrow-eyed expression. Clearing his throat, he carefully pulled off the gloves.

"You're right," said Denzel. "That's really quite dangerous." He smiled. "Anything else you want to show me?"

"Yeah," said Boyle, through gritted teeth. "I can think of something." He handed Denzel a piece of plastic the size of a credit card.

"What's this?" asked Denzel. "A secret laser? A ghost-exploding-thing?"

"It's a key," said Boyle "To your room. Number's on the back."

Denzel blinked. "What?"

"Go. Relax. Check out your quarters," said Boyle, ushering Denzel towards the door. "The longer you spend in there, the safer we'll all be out here."

"But…"

"Psht!" hissed Boyle, holding a finger to his lips. "Talk later. Go to quarters now. Oh, and Denzel?"

"Yeah?"

"Try not to damage any multi-billion pound pieces of equipment along the way."

Denzel wandered through the corridors, headed in what he hoped was the direction of the living quarters. He passed a handful of people in uniforms and robes, but they all looked far too busy for him to go bothering them with questions.

The corridor turned off into a stairwell, with a set of metal steps leading up and down. Denzel searched the walls, hoping for something that would indicate in which direction he should be going, but there were no signs or notices, and he quickly drew a blank.

He was halfway through deciding which way to choose using his tried-and-tested "eenie, meenie, miney, mo" decision-making method, when he heard a voice he recognised. The echo of the stairwell meant he couldn't tell whether it was coming from above or below, but there was no mistaking the voice's owner.

"Yes, he's quite fascinating," said Quinn. "I don't yet know how he does what he does, but we'll find out. One way or another."

"You really think he'll make a collector?" asked another voice. It was a girl, but not Samara. This voice was much gruffer. The girl who'd pointed the gun at him in the lift, Denzel guessed. Knightley, wasn't it?

"I don't see why not," said Quinn. She was growing louder now as she drew closer. Denzel looked up and down, but still couldn't figure out where the sound was coming from. "I'm hoping he'll fit in nicely."

"And if he doesn't?" the girl asked. "What then?"

The footsteps stopped and silence fell. Denzel held his breath, waiting for Quinn's answer.

"Hello, Denzel," she said, her voice echoing around him. "Are you lost?"

"Uh, yeah," said Denzel. "I'm trying to find my room."

Quinn and Knightley appeared at the top of the staircase and made their way down. "Yes, it can be quite confusing at first," Quinn said. "How is it all going?"

"Uh, good," said Denzel. "I'm learning, you know, things."

"Excellent. Keep it up," said Quinn. "Third door on the left, straight on, then a right."

Denzel frowned. "What?"

"Your room," said Quinn. "Out the door, third door on the left, straight on, then a right. You can't miss it. I can have Knightley escort you, if you wish?"

Denzel glanced across at the girl. She glared back at him with barely concealed distaste. "Uh, no, I'll find it," he said, backing towards the door. "Thanks."

"Don't mention it," said Quinn. "Oh, and Denzel?"

"Yeah?"

"I spoke to your parents," Quinn said. "Lovely couple, very proud of you. We had a chat and everything has been taken care of."

"Oh. Right, cool," said Denzel. "What did you tell them?"

"No need to dwell on the details. Everything has been taken care of." Quinn smiled her not-quite smile. "Trust me."

"Uh, OK," said Denzel, then he backed through the door and scurried off to find his room.

CHAPTER 10

Despite Quinn's directions, it took Denzel another twenty minutes of searching before he finally found the living quarters, and five more before he found his room.

Although "room" was stretching it a bit. "Cell" would have been a more fitting description. It had grey walls, a grey carpet, a grey ceiling and a bed made of metal. Also grey. The only splash of colour was the single pillow, which was a sort of greyish-white. Compared to the rest of the room, it looked positively festive.

Denzel threw himself on to the bed – which turned out to be painfully firm – and lay on his back staring blankly upwards. He imagined the millions of tonnes of soil that lay between him and the world above, and tried, without much success, not to feel claustrophobic.

For a long time, he didn't move. His mind raced back over everything that had happened in the past few hours. He'd evaded a trash-monster, come face-to-face with a poltergeist, used magic, and quite possibly destroyed a state-of-the-art robotic battle suit. All in all, it had been a pretty eventful day.

It was amazing. All of it. Absolutely incredible.

And yet...

He couldn't help thinking about his old ceiling back home. It was mostly white, with some little yellow blotches from the time he'd tried to open a bottle of banana milkshake and accidentally exploded it everywhere. Denzel smiled at the memory, then felt a pang of something in his chest.

He wondered what his dads were doing. Had Quinn explained his absence in a way that hadn't left them worried? He wished he'd pressed her for an explanation, and hoped they weren't pacing the floor in panic. Would he be in trouble when he got home?

Because he *was* going home. Despite the ghosts, magic and giant robots, despite how cool the idea of being part of a secret society of spook hunters was, Denzel knew he wasn't going to stay. Exciting as this new life might be, he couldn't just turn his back on his old one.

There was a knock at the door. Denzel swung his legs out of bed and opened the door to find Samara standing outside.

"Hi!" she said brightly. "You hungry?"

"Uh, yeah," said Denzel. It had been a long time since his half-sandwich, and his stomach was quietly grumbling its impatience.

"Great!" Samara smiled that smile of hers, and bowed. "Then perhaps you would do me the honour of joining me for dinner?"

"Dinner?" said Denzel, his voice wobbling. "What, like, you and me?"

"Yep, you and me," said Samara. "And Boyle, of course."

"Oh. Yeah. Can't forget Boyle," said Denzel, trying to hide his disappointment.

"Come on, I'll show you the dinner hall," said Samara. "But I should probably warn you, it can be a little overwhelming."

"It can't be any worse than my school canteen."

"Oh," said Samara. "I think it probably can."

Denzel stared at the canteen in disbelief. "You're right," he said, shouting to make himself heard over the din.

"This is worse."

The canteen looked like … well, like pretty much any other canteen. There were forty or more long folding tables, each with room for eight people to sit and eat. From what Denzel could gather, the room was pretty much split in two, with Oberons over on the left, and Vulterons on the right.

The Vulteron side was filled with people zooming around on Segways, clanking about on exoskeleton feet, or generally just strutting around like they owned the place. Most of the hundred and fifty or so people in that half of the room wore the standard blue and silver camo, but a few were dressed in all-blue boiler suits that zipped up at the front.

Pacing through the throngs of Vulterons were at least two robots. They were roughly human shape and size, and carried trays in their perfectly balanced hands. Denzel had no idea if they were delivering food to someone, or planning to eat it themselves, and as the other Vulterons crossed from the queue to the tables, the robots were lost in the crowd.

Over on the other side of the dining hall, the Oberons were using magic. At least, Denzel guessed they were, as he could think of no other explanation for all the trays that floated around the place before landing on the tables in front of the waiting diners.

Some of the tables were floating, too. In fact, the Oberon side of the room looked far more spacious, as at least a third of the tables were hovering in the air several metres above the others, creating a sort of double-decker dining effect.

Everyone seemed to be talking at the same time. The Vulterons were barking at each other, like they were locked in some sort of who's-got-the-gruffest-voice competition. The Oberons below were calling to those above, while those above were shouting down for someone to chuck them up the salt.

"It's massive," said Denzel. "There's so many of them. Of you, I mean."

"Yeah, this branch is the base for most of northern Europe," Samara said. "There's a little outpost up in the north of Scotland, and a couple dotted around France and Spain, but this is the biggest outside the United States."

"The United States?" said Denzel. "Of America?"

"Yeah, unless there's another United States no one's told me about. It's a worldwide organisation. You can find us pretty much everywhere, if you know where to look."

"Right. Wow," said Denzel, because he couldn't really

think of anything more interesting to add.

"Come on, let's go and get something to eat," said Samara, guiding him along by the sleeve. They dodged their way through the throngs towards the Oberon queue. It was far shorter than the line of Vulterons on the other side of the hall, largely because everyone was just magically summoning their trays to their tables, rather than lining up in an orderly fashion.

Denzel ducked to avoid a bowl of rice pudding that came whooshing past him like a flying saucer, then joined Samara at the serving counter. It was set out pretty much exactly like a school canteen, with a glass cabinet protecting six metal tubs, all containing different types of food.

"OK, so we've got chicken curry, vegetarian chilli, pizza, but that looks a bit dry, so I'd probably avoid that, and some sort of pasta thing with broccoli in it," said Samara, handing him a tray. "Oh, and there's always baked potatoes, too. You can have any filling you want, as long as it's cheese or tuna. Anything take your fancy?"

"Is that it?" Denzel asked, then he realised it had come out wrong. "I mean, this all looks great, but I thought..."

"Thought what?" asked Samara.

"Just that it'd be, you know, like ... weirder," Denzel said. "Like there'd be, I don't know, dragon or something."

"Dragon?" Samara snorted.

"Yeah. Or something."

"Nah. Dragon's on Tuesdays," Samara said, and the way she smiled meant Denzel couldn't tell if she was joking or not. "Now, hurry up and choose something. I'm starving!"

Before Denzel could pick anything, Boyle appeared. "Samara," he grunted. "We're up."

"What? But I thought..." Samara glanced back at Denzel. "What about his training?"

"The director wants us to bring him," Boyle said. He didn't look happy about that at all, but closed his mouth before he could say any more.

"I'll probably just have pizza," Denzel announced, but then Boyle yanked the tray from his hand and deposited it back in the pile.

"No. You won't," said Boyle. "We've got a call."

Denzel looked between Boyle and Samara, not quite sure what Boyle was getting at. "Like ... a phone call?"

"Like a call-out," said Samara. "A mission. We're being sent to deal with a situation."

Denzel swallowed. "A ghost situation?"

"It'll be fine, don't worry about it," said Samara. "Just think of it as some on-the-job training."

Her eyes flicked to her partner. "Besides, it's not like

Quinn would let us take you out on anything *major*, right?" She watched Boyle's expression closely. "Right?"

"Well," said Boyle. "It's funny you should ask..."

CHAPTER 11

Denzel screamed and threw himself to the ground, just as something fast, white and very, *very* angry hurtled past him.

It was a ghost. Not a litter-monster, not a smoky octopus – a proper, old-fashioned eyeholes-in-a-sheet type ghost!

And, to Denzel's dismay, it was not alone. There were dozens of the things, screeching and flailing around as they swooped, dived at – and passed straight through – the shelves of the supermarket Denzel was cowering in.

Chains rattled somewhere along the aisle. Denzel looked up to see a semi-transparent skeleton stalking past the baby food and nappies, dragging a set of ghostly shackles behind him.

Above the skeleton's head, something that could feasibly have been a net curtain with a face drawn on let out an unearthly moan, then knocked over a carefully balanced display of baby wipes as it went flying past.

A crackle of magic or gunfire or something else dangerous-sounding echoed from the next aisle over. The breakfast cereal section, Denzel guessed, judging by the snap, crackle and pop that followed the blast.

A decaying ghostly hand appeared through the floor beside Denzel, its withered fingers grabbing at him. Denzel heard himself scream again, then kicked forwards, using the shelving to heave himself to his feet.

He clattered down the aisle, the screeching and rattling sounding as if it were right behind him. At the bottom, he skidded around the corner and came face-to-snarl with Knightley. She snapped up her rifle and he had to throw his hands up to stop her shooting.

"Wait, not a ghost, not a ghost!"

"Well, get out of my way," Knightley hissed, then she fired a blast of searing white energy over his head at something big and almost certainly terrifying that had been right behind him. Denzel felt his head get hot and smelled his hair singe. He ducked and ran, then threw himself over a grocery conveyor belt, and landed, upside down, behind a checkout.

Something white flew at his face and he screamed again. A full three seconds passed before he realised it was just a carrier bag.

With some effort, Denzel managed to turn himself right way up. He kept low, peeking just the very top of his head above the checkout. A dozen or more shapeless white apparitions floated up near the ceiling. From four different aisles, four different energy blasts screamed towards them, courtesy of Boyle, Samara, Knightley and Knightley's partner, Rasmus.

Denzel had been introduced to Rasmus, a tall, spotty-faced Oberon, at the mission briefing. Rasmus had immediately made his dislike of Denzel abundantly clear, and warned him not to get in his way.

Denzel had promised he wouldn't, then accidentally stood on Rasmus's robe almost at once, tripping him up. Samara had laughed about it, but no one else seemed to see the funny side, Rasmus in particular.

The actual briefing was a bit of a blur. Quinn had mentioned something about a supermarket extension disturbing an old burial ground, but there'd be a lot of talk of *Free-Floating* this and *Class Two* that, and Denzel hadn't paid too much attention. As far as he knew, he was tagging along to watch, and he hadn't expected to be caught in the middle of a full-scale ghost battle.

A beam of fizzing purple power struck one of the sheet-like ghosts right in the flappy parts. The ghost clawed at the air for a moment, then was yanked sharply down behind some shelving.

"Got one!" called Boyle.

A hail of short, pulsing energy bolts erupted from the next aisle over. Two ghosts spun as they were hit, then dropped to the floor like wounded birds.

"Nailed *two*," Knightley shouted. "Rasmus, gem them up!"

"On it!"

"Try not to make a mess of it, Rasmus." That was Samara's voice. "Just shout if you need help."

"Oh, *shut up*," Rasmus spat.

Denzel's heart, which had been thudding like a jackhammer, began to slow. Things seemed to be in hand. The ghosts were dropping, the Spectre Collectors were still standing, and it looked like everything was going to be OK.

Besides, no one had seen him ducking behind the checkout. He was hidden down there. Hidden and safe.

THWANG!

The drawer of the checkout's till sprung open,

smacking Denzel on the forehead. "Ow!" he grimaced, then he watched in horror as two ghostly hands crept out of the cash drawer, the fingers wrapping like insect-legs around the edges.

"Boo!" cackled a hollow-eyed head as it popped out of the drawer, scattering notes and coins all over the floor. A gust of cold air rolled over Denzel as he jumped to his feet and half-climbed, half-fell out from behind the checkout desk.

"B-back off," Denzel stammered. He held his fingers in front of him in the shape of a cross, even though he was pretty sure that only worked on vampires, and even then, only in movies. "Don't come any closer, or I'll... I'll...."

He would what? Scream? Run away? Wet himself? All those things were possible, certainly, but the sight of the ghost emerging from behind the checkout and fluttering towards him had turned his legs and brain to jelly, and he couldn't decide what his next course of action should be.

Denzel had just decided to try all three of those tactics at the same time when a black circle, about the size of a large car tyre, appeared in the air above the ghost. The spook looked up just as a hand reached down through the hole and grabbed hold of it.

"Not so fast, sunshine!" said a voice Denzel recognised as Samara's. The ghost's empty eyes widened as it was yanked up into the darkness.

A moment later, Samara leaned down through the hole and shot Denzel a smile. "You all right?"

"Uh... Uh... Uh..." was all Denzel managed to say.

"Good stuff. Won't be long. Shout if you need us," said Samara. She gave him a thumbs-up, then winced as a tin of soup dropped out of the hole and *thonked* her on the back of the head. "Oi, watch it!" she warned, before withdrawing back into the hole, which promptly sealed itself shut.

Cautiously, Denzel approached the spot where the hole had been, and swished his arms around. Nothing. It was as if it had never been there.

Samara shouted something to Boyle, but her voice was far away, already at the other end of the hangar-sized supermarket.

"This is crazy," Denzel whispered, shuffling around in a circle as he watched for trouble.

There were no ghosts lurking nearby – or none he could see, at least. The battle was still sparking and whooshing and flashing like an indoor fireworks display. Every few seconds Denzel's skin would tingle or his stomach would flip or his hair would stand on end in time with one of the blasts, as he felt its effects all the way at the other end of the supermarket.

After one particularly acrobatic flip, his stomach rumbled hungrily. There was a stack of chocolate bars next to the nearest till. Denzel thought about wolfing one down, but he didn't have any money to pay for it.

Of course, considering a large area of the supermarket was in the process of being blasted to pieces by ghost-hunting equipment and magic, one missing Twix was unlikely to be a big issue.

But it would still be wrong.

And yet he was absolutely starving, now that he thought about it.

And now that he'd thought about it, he couldn't *stop* thinking about it.

He was trying to navigate his way through this moral maze when he heard a voice.

"Help!"

It was soft and quiet, and belonged to an old woman. Denzel knew it belonged to an old woman because it had that certain distinctive tremble to it that you only ever found in the voices of old women.

Also, there was an old woman half-crouching behind the newspaper stand, waving to him.

Denzel waved back. Then he realised she probably

wasn't being friendly, and was trying to get his attention.

Sure enough. "Please! H-help!"

Glancing over his shoulder, Denzel hoped he'd seen someone more qualified who could go and see what the lady wanted, but there was nothing there but the display of chocolate bars and – far beyond it – the ongoing ghost battle.

"Please!"

"All right, all right, hold your horses," Denzel muttered. He ducked as low as he could without actually collapsing to the floor and ran in short bursts towards the newspaper stand.

It took him a little longer than expected to get there, because every few steps or so he got paranoid a ghost was about to jump on his back, and he was forced to keep stopping and spinning on the spot to check.

When he finally made it to the rack, the old woman almost burst into tears. "What's going on?" she asked, her voice even more wobbly up close. "What's happening?" She stared up at him from where she sat on the floor, her eyes wide, imploring, searching for hope.

Denzel opened his mouth to say, "It's a load of ghosts," then decided the shock of that might kill her. Instead, he said, "Mice."

If he were honest, he hadn't been expecting to say

"mice", and he had to hurriedly rearrange his expression to stop the woman noticing his surprise.

"Mice?"

"Yep," said Denzel, sounding pretty squeaky himself. "There are mice. In the shop."

"Grenade!" shouted Knightley. At the far end of the store, something exploded.

"Big ones. *Very* aggressive," Denzel added. He looked behind him to the supermarket's front door, then back to the trembling pensioner. "We were told everyone had been evacuated. How come you're still here?"

"I was in the toilet," the old woman began, then she launched into a short but detailed description of her bowel movements, which Denzel managed to tune out by focusing on the sounds of gunfire and ghost howls. He tuned in again in time to hear, "...And after I'd *finally* got it to flush, I came out to find all this going on."

"OK, OK, that's all ... very vivid, thanks," said Denzel. "Can you run to the door?"

"I've got two plastic hips," the woman said.

"Right. Can you *walk* to the door?"

The woman's eyes shone with tears. "I don't... I'm not... Will you help me?"

Denzel peeked up over the newspaper rack to make sure nothing horrible was approaching, then smiled at the woman. "Yeah. Yeah, of course I will. Come on."

With some difficulty, a lot of awkwardness, and several "up you get"s, Denzel managed to haul the old lady to her feet. She clung to his arm, letting him take some of her weight. She wasn't much taller than he was, and the fingers around his arm felt mostly bone, so there wasn't a lot of weight to take. As they shuffled slowly towards the exit he was almost tempted just to throw her over his shoulder and make a run for it.

Eventually, they reached the supermarket's door. It slid open at their approach, and Denzel guided the woman towards the opening. "Almost there," he said. "Easy does it. Just a few more—"

THUD!

An invisible barrier blocked the doorway. "What's the matter, love?" the old woman asked, as Denzel reached up and pressed his hand against the wall of solid air. The street was right there, right on the other side, but the barrier prevented them leaving the shop.

"They've blocked it," Denzel groaned. "They've blocked us in here with magic."

"Who has?" asked the woman.

Denzel turned to her, realised he'd been speaking out loud, and tried a hasty cover-up. "Er, the mice," he said.

"The mice have blocked us in with magic?"

"Yes. They're more cunning than people realise," Denzel said. He was about to turn away and look for somewhere to take cover, when something about the street caught his attention.

In fact, that wasn't quite true. Something about it had caught his attention before then, but it was at that moment that he realised what that something was. It was deserted. The street – the entire city centre street – was empty. Not a pedestrian. Not a car. Not even a bird in the sky. Empty pavements, *empty* roads, just empty, full stop.

"Huh, that's weird," Denzel said, then he shuffled around with the old woman and almost screamed again when he saw a figure in black standing in the middle of the supermarket foyer.

"Hello, Denzel," said Director Quinn.

Denzel started to reply, but Quinn held up a hand and motioned for silence. "I'll explain later. For now, please step away from the old lady."

The woman's grip tightened on Denzel's arm. "Who's she? Where did she come from?" the woman asked.

"She's fine, she's... Don't panic, it's nothing to worry about."

"Denzel. Step away," Quinn said, and Denzel noticed the director had one hand tucked behind her back, out of sight. A faint shimmer of blue light fizzled along the fingertips of her other hand.

"Um…" Denzel swallowed. "Is she…?"

Quinn nodded.

"Right," said Denzel. "Because she doesn't look like…"

"No. But she is," said Quinn.

"Don't look like what?" asked the old lady. Her grip tightened further on Denzel's arm until he felt like her bony fingers were going to dig into his flesh. The skin felt cold, even through his clothes. "What don't I look like?"

"Uh… Like you've had a drink in a while," said Denzel. "I'll go and get you some water."

He tried to pull his arm away, but the woman's grip was like a vice clamped around him. The old lady began to laugh, a high-pitched witchy shriek that came mostly through her nose.

"Denzel, step away," Quinn instructed, her voice clipped and urgent.

"Trying!" Denzel said, gritting his teeth and heaving against the cackling pensioner's grip. "Can't … break … free!"

Quinn didn't panic or shout or look in any way like she was under stress. She just tutted and sighed, like she'd done this one too many times before.

She brought the hand out from behind her back. It was

holding a futuristic-looking pistol with a barrel the size of a tin can. The old woman stopped laughing as Quinn took aim at her forehead and squeezed the trigger.

There was a *whumpf* sound, like a tiny thunderclap, and what had until very recently been a pensioner's head became a snarling, thrashing mass of ghostly tentacles.

"Um…" said Denzel, now trying even more frantically to free his trapped arm. "Um… Um…"

"Don't worry, Denzel, it's all under control," said Quinn. She pushed forwards with her empty hand and the tentacle-headed old lady flew backwards and slammed against the invisible barrier.

The woman – or whatever it was – slid to the floor and lay still. Quinn muttered something below her breath, then smiled at Denzel.

"Walk with me a moment," she said. "You look like you could use some fresh air."

Denzel followed Quinn towards the door, being sure to give the motionless tentacle-lady as wide a berth as possible. As they neared the spot where Denzel knew the barrier to be, Quinn held a hand out to him.

After a moment, he took it. The air seemed to ripple around them as Denzel was led out through the front door.

The noise caught him off-guard. Honking. Engines.

Snapshots of conversations. The sounds of a busy city street.

And it *was* busy. Pedestrians passed the door in their hundreds. Cars, vans and buses were snarled in the road, with the occasional cyclist whizzing smugly past them.

Denzel looked back towards the supermarket door. "But... But... None of this was here a minute ago."

"Yes, it was," said Quinn, inhaling deeply through her nose. "It's always here. All ... this." She gestured around at the packed city centre, and Denzel thought he saw her nostrils flaring with distaste. "We surround each incident with ... well, let's call it a bubble. It keeps the outside world at bay while we get on with the task at hand."

"But how?" said Denzel. "I mean, the shop's still there. The door's open. What if someone walks in?"

"They never do," said Quinn. She nodded along the pavement. "Observe."

Denzel watched as a harassed-looking woman with three children and a "Bag for Life" approached the supermarket front door, looked briefly confused, then diverted and carried on along the street.

"She doesn't know why she did that," Quinn explained, as the woman walked off. "She had every intention of going inside, but something told her not to. Something that affected her on a fundamental, primal level, but without her even noticing."

"You can do that to people?" Denzel asked.

"Ha!" said Quinn, but without any real humour in it. "People are easy. With a bit of effort, you can make anyone do or think whatever you want." She turned away from the noise and the traffic and looked at Denzel for the first time since they'd left the shop. "Or you *could*, were you so inclined."

She turned away again, and looked both ways along the pavement. "Look at them. They have no idea about the dangers lurking beneath the surface of this world. They have no idea what we do to keep them safe." She rocked on her heels and clicked her tongue against the roof of her mouth. "I used to envy them that. Their ignorance."

"And now?" asked Denzel.

Quinn didn't say anything for a few seconds. Instead, she about-turned and took Denzel's hand again. "Now I pity them," she said, then the sound of the city was replaced by the howling of ghosts and the crackle of magic as they stepped back inside the shop.

The old woman was no longer lying on the floor. That was the first thing Denzel noticed. The next thing he noticed was that she was clinging to the ceiling like Spider-Man, her tentacle head whipping at the air.

"I thought you said you had plastic hips!" Denzel cried. Beside him, Quinn raised a hand and muttered something below her breath. The ceiling tiles rippled like water, and the ghost lost its grip.

Denzel leapt clear as the old woman's body hit the floor with a damp-sounding *thwap*. "Ooh, that had to hurt," he whispered, then he yelped in fright as one of her hands pulled itself free from her sleeve and began scurrying towards him on its fingertips.

The tentacle head made a grab for Quinn, forcing her backwards. Denzel hopped and stamped his foot as the hand scrambled for him. "Argh! Back off! Stop it!"

The fingers crouched low at the knuckles, then the hand launched itself at him like a jumping spider. It landed on his chest, and he frantically tried to flick it away. "Aah! Get off!" he yelped, but the hand darted around his back, and up on to his shoulder.

"Help!" he cried, but Quinn was busy dodging the old woman's tentacle-head. Denzel hissed as the hand yanked his hair and sent him stumbling into a rack of tabloid newspapers.

"Ow, ow, ow!" he protested. He grabbed for the hand and heaved at it, but only succeeded in pulling his own hair. "Ooh, worse, worse, worse!"

He spun. He twisted. He dug his fingernails into the

detached hand's wrist, but with no effect.

"Denzel, don't move!" barked a familiar voice. Completely ignoring the suggestion, he turned to find Boyle and Knightley both closing in on him, guns raised. "You've got something in your hair."

"I *know* I've got something in my hair!" Denzel cried. "Get it out of my hair."

"Done!" sneered Knightley, looking along the sight of her rifle.

"No, wait!" said Boyle, but then Knightley's gun let out a loud, high-pitched screech. Denzel felt a sensation, like the whole world had taken one step to the left and not bothered to tell him.

And everything went dark.

CHAPTER 12

Denzel woke with a start. Or, more accurately, a scream.

He spent a panicky few seconds thrashing and kicking, and it was only thanks to some impressively fast reflexes that Director Quinn managed to avoid a flailing fist to the face.

"Ah, there you are," she said from the bottom of his bed, once he'd stopped trying to beat up thin air. "We were starting to worry you were never going to wake up."

Denzel's hands shot to his hair. He was relieved to find nothing holding on to it, and let out a breath he seemed to have been holding even in his sleep.

"How long was I out for?" he asked.

"About nine hours," said Samara. She was sitting in a chair near the head of the bed. She smiled as Denzel noticed her, then unscrewed the cap on a bottle of water and passed it to him. "You went down pretty hard."

Denzel took a gulp of the water, then pressed the cool plastic against his cheek. "Did Knightley shoot me?"

"She shot *near* you," said Quinn. "Too near, obviously. She has been reprimanded."

"Right. OK. I suppose that's fair enough, then," said Denzel. He cricked his neck, then smoothed down his hair. "What was that thing? The old woman, I mean."

"Not really an old woman, for one," said Quinn.

"Yeah, I guessed that," said Denzel. "You know, with the way her head turned into an octopus, and everything."

"Well spotted," said Quinn. "If you want to get technical about it, it was a Corporeal Four-Dimensional Non-Mortal Entity."

Denzel went through all those words in his head, trying to figure out what any of them meant. One phrase jumped out. "Four-Dimensional?"

"It means they're fully formed in the physical realm, and are also capable of tactile interaction," said Samara.

Denzel nodded. "Right. And in English...?"

"*Three*-dimensional Corporeals look like they're really

121

there, but can't touch you," Quinn explained. "Four-dimensional ones can."

"And you don't want to know about the five-dimensional ones," said Samara. "Trust me."

"So ... it's a ghost?" said Denzel.

"Yes," said Quinn.

"But it's solid?"

"Yes," said Samara.

"Then, I mean... How is it a ghost?" Denzel asked. "I mean, the other ones – the things that looked like sheets? They're ghosts, I get that. But that old woman looked just like ... well, like an old woman. To start with, anyway."

"In some ways, she *was* an old woman," said Quinn. "Or as close to one as it's possible to be, at least, without actually being one. If that makes sense?"

"Not really," said Denzel.

Quinn smiled her not-quite smile. "Even our equipment can't always detect a Corporeal. We have no idea how many are out there, living among us. Well, not *living*, obviously. Existing. Luckily for you I was observing. I wanted to see how you'd do out in the field."

"And how did I do?" Denzel asked, although he could probably guess.

"You're alive," said Quinn. "That's a pretty positive

result. There's no saying what the Corporeal might have done to you, had I not intervened."

"She didn't really seem to be trying to hurt me or anything," Denzel said. "She just said she wanted my help."

He thought back to the poltergeist, and those two words snaking in the air.

"Yes, well, they'll say anything," Quinn said. "They can't be trusted."

She smoothed the cover of Denzel's bed, then stood up. "Anyway, good to see you awake. Samara, please make sure Denzel has everything he needs, then best leave him to rest." She smiled down at Denzel. "I want you wide awake for training tomorrow."

"But ... I'm going home tomorrow," said Denzel.

"Twenty-four hours. That's what you promised us," said Quinn, heading for the door. "So training. With Boyle. Tomorrow morning."

Samara stood up and did something that was sort of half a bow and half a curtsey to the director, then the door closed, leaving the two of them alone.

"I'm *really* sorry about what happened," Samara said. "It's my fault. I should've been keeping a closer watch on you."

"It's fine, don't worry about it. You had ghosts to catch

and all that stuff," said Denzel. "Get them all?"

"Yeah, we got them," Samara replied. "Well, except the Corporeal. It got away. The others are all gemmed up and locked in Spectral Storage."

"And what happens to them then?" Denzel asked, shimmying himself into an upright position on the bed. "What do you do with them? Do you send them to the Spectre Realm?"

"Spectral Realm, and no," said Samara. "For that, we'd have to open a gateway, and that's too dangerous."

"How do they get out? From the Spectral Realm, I mean?" Denzel asked. "That's how they get here, right?"

Samara shook her head. "No. Once something's in there, we don't think it can get out. It's a one-way street. The ghosts that show up here on this side have never found their way to the Spectral Realm, for some reason. Or have decided they prefer it here, maybe."

"And you just keep them locked up?" said Denzel. "Forever?"

Samara stood up. "Well, it's that or we let them go free," she said, shrugging. "And you've seen what happens then."

"Yeah. Suppose," said Denzel. "Sounds like whatever Quinn's got planned will make life more simple for everyone."

Samara turned. "Got planned?"

"Yeah. To get rid of all the ghosts, or something?" Denzel said. "Said the Spectre Collectors wouldn't be needed after that."

Samara nodded slowly. "Right. Yeah. Of course. Did she say anything else?"

"No," said Denzel. "No, I don't think so... Um, except, now I think about it, when she asked me to keep it to myself."

"Don't worry, I won't tell her you told me," Samara said. She hung back for a moment, like she was about to say something else, but then shook her head. "Goodnight, Denzel."

"Night," said Denzel, as Samara left and closed the door.

He slid back down in the bed, too tired to even take off his clothes. He needed the toilet. It wasn't a pressing urge, but he knew if he fell asleep now he'd wake up with his bladder screaming at him in a couple of hours.

He should go find the bathroom. It wouldn't be far away.

Yes, he thought, closing his eyes, he should definitely go and find the bathroom.

Next morning, Denzel woke up not needing the toilet at

all. At first, he panicked that he'd wet himself during the night, but was relieved to discover the sheets were bone dry.

He *did* almost wet himself a few moments later, however, when Boyle came bursting into his room, shouting at him to get up and get ready for training.

Denzel stood across from Boyle now, chewing on a cereal bar and gazing down at the gun in his hand, quietly trying to figure out where the trigger was. It wasn't that he couldn't see a trigger on it, it was more that he could see too many of them. There were three sticking out of various parts of the barrel, and at least another one tucked round the back.

"Get all that?" asked Boyle.

Denzel swallowed the last of the cereal bar and looked up. "Hmm?"

Boyle twitched with irritation. "Did you get everything I just said?"

"I got the general gist of it," Denzel lied. "But it might be worth going over it again, just to be on the safe side."

Boyle shook his head and muttered below his breath. "OK, short version," he snapped. "As you saw yesterday, ghosts come in lots of different forms. Some are invisible – to most of us, anyway – some are semi-transparent, some are glowing balls of energy, some are solid, whatever…"

"I still don't get how they can be solid," said Denzel.

"Because they're supernatural spirit energy, they can be whatever they want," Boyle said. "Which reminds me. Did you take the Plasmic Disruptor yesterday?"

"Not that I know of," said Denzel. "What is it?"

"That box you picked up when I was showing you the Spook Suit," said Boyle, his eyes narrowing. "You seemed awfully interested in it, and now it's gone."

"Oh. No," said Denzel. "Why would I take it?"

"You tell me," said Boyle.

"Well … I can't, because I didn't take it," said Denzel.

Boyle advanced. "Is that right?"

"Uh, yes. That's right."

Boyle stopped just a few centimetres closer than Denzel was completely comfortable with. Denzel could hear Boyle's breath going in and out through his nose as the Vulteron glared down at him.

"Fair enough, then," Boyle finally said. He stepped back and gestured to the gun in Denzel's hands. "The Mark 4 Vapourshaker. Standard kit for agents in the field, before it was replaced by the newer model. Still an effective piece of weaponry, though."

"It looks it," said Denzel. "With all the triggers and

knobbly bits and everything."

"*Knobbly bits?*" Boyle scowled, then he shook his head and continued. "Forget it, doesn't matter. Just point and shoot, it's all set up."

He indicated a door at the other end of the small room. There was a window beside it, showing a theatre-style street scene set on the other side, complete with painted city backdrop and a couple of two-dimensional bins made of wood standing in front.

"Head through there and wait for the targets to pop up. Once you're sure they're ghosts, you open fire. If they aren't ghosts, or you're not sure, you don't. Got it?"

Denzel nodded. "Got it. Shoot the ghosts, don't shoot the other stuff."

He stepped through the door and it swung closed behind him. Boyle appeared at the window. "OK, beginning program," he said. "Good luck."

Denzel clutched the gun close to him, his finger on one of its many triggers. His eyes darted around the set, searching for some clue as to where the ghosts were going to come from. "I can do this," he whispered.

There was a sudden movement from behind the bin, and something terrifying snapped up on a spring.

Denzel screamed, shut his eyes, then opened fire.

SPECTRE COLLECTORS

"So, how did it go?"

Director Quinn sat behind her desk, her fingers steepled in front of her. Denzel stood between Samara and Boyle, shuffling awkwardly.

"It didn't go *brilliantly*," he admitted.

"He shot a little girl in the face," said Boyle.

"Accidentally," said Denzel.

"Eleven times," added Boyle.

"Not a real little girl, though, just a cardboard cut-out."

"Ah. I see," said Quinn, leaning back in her chair. She turned her attention to Samara. "Any more luck with you?"

"Not really," Samara said. "I tried him with a Feurety Ring, but it didn't go well."

"How 'not well'?"

"He almost set me on fire."

Quinn nodded. "I see," she said. "Still, not to worry. I'm convinced you can fit in here, Denzel. We just have to—"

"No," said Denzel.

Quinn's smile faltered. "I'm sorry?"

"I mean, thanks for the offer and everything, it's been really interesting, but I think I'd like to go home now."

"Home?" said Quinn, as if it was a word she wasn't familiar with.

"Yeah," said Denzel. "You know? Home."

For a long time, no one spoke. Denzel had just reached the point of feeling so uncomfortable he was about to say something himself, when Quinn nodded. "Of course," she said, standing up. She held a hand out. "It's a shame it didn't work out. I think we could've learned a lot from each other, Denzel, but you must do what you feel is right, of course."

"Uh, thanks," said Denzel, shaking the director's hand. "Do you have to, like, wipe my memory now or something?"

"That won't be necessary," said Quinn.

"What?" said Boyle. "But—"

Quinn held a hand up to silence him. "That won't be necessary. Denzel can go. I trust him to keep our secrets." She was still holding Denzel's hand, and tightened her grip on it as she leaned closer. "We can trust you, can't we, Denzel?"

"Yeah. Yeah, of course."

"Good," she said. "Then I wish you all the best, and pray that the Allwhere may always watch over you."

"Uh, OK. Thanks. I guess I'll be off, then," he said. "Oh, but I meant to ask… My dads?"

"What about them?"

"When you told them I wasn't going to be home, what

did you say?"

"Don't worry about it. That's not important," said Quinn. "The important thing is, it won't pose you any problems. In fact," she added, her smile returning, "I'd be very surprised if they even noticed you were gone."

CHAPTER 13

Denzel stepped out of the lift and blinked in the mid-morning sunshine. The air felt cool and sharp against his skin. He breathed it in deeply, enjoying the freshness of it.

Stepping round the corner, he collided with someone lurking right on the other side. "Wah! Get off!" Smithy yelped, swishing his arms around wildly. He stopped when he realised who had bumped into him. "Denzel! It's you! You're alive!"

"Of course I'm alive," said Denzel. "What are you doing here? Have you been here since yesterday?"

"Of course not! I definitely haven't spent the whole

night just wandering around a creepy old church, no siree," said Smithy. "I was just coming to check on you, in case you were in danger or anything."

Denzel shook his head. "Thanks, but I wasn't in danger. Shouldn't you be at school?"

"Yeah, but so should you," Smithy pointed out.

"Director Quinn said she'd sorted it so I don't get into trouble," said Denzel.

"That's handy," said Smithy. "Did she sort it for me, too?"

"I doubt it," said Denzel.

Smithy shrugged. "Ah well. Want to hang out?"

Denzel yawned. "Hmm? Oh, no, not right now, sorry. I'm exhausted. And starving."

"I've still got some scrambled egg, if you want," said Smithy, pulling the crinkled paper bag from his pocket.

"No, I'm all right, ta," said Denzel. "I think I'll just head home."

"Oh. OK," said Smithy, folding the bag up again. "Hey, Denzel, here's one for you..." he began, but Denzel stopped him.

"Not now, Smithy," said Denzel.

Smithy's smile faded. "Oh. Yeah. OK."

"It's just... It's been a bit of a weird couple of days."

"Yeah. Of course," said Smithy. He rallied his smile.

"See you at school on Monday?"

"Yeah. Definitely. See you at school," Denzel said, then, with a final wave to his friend, he turned and hurried around the side of the church.

Wiggins Street, where the church was, was on the opposite side of town to his house. A bus would get him home before his dads got in, and so avoid lots of awkward questions, but he didn't have any money on him.

He decided just to run. He darted along Wiggins Street and weaved through the leafy housing estate it stood on the edge of. He speed-walked through the more densely packed town centre. Now he was further away from the church and surrounded by people, the underground bunker had begun to feel like a strange dream.

By the time he turned on to his road twenty minutes later, he had a spring in his step. Yes, he'd been attacked by a giant litter-monster, had several guns pointed at him, almost been snared by a rampaging poltergeist, been hit on the head by a haunted supermarket till and come face-to-tentacles with a terrifying ghost-pensioner, but all that was behind him now. It had been a mad couple of days, but tomorrow was the weekend and, statistically, it was more or less guaranteed to be better.

Even the sight of his dads' car outside the house

didn't dampen his mood. If anything, it made his smile widen. He wasn't sure what Quinn had said to them, and probably should have pressed her for an explanation, but she seemed pretty persuasive. If anything, he might just get a bit of a telling-off, and he wasn't too bothered about that. He'd welcome a telling-off, in fact. A telling-off was normal, and a healthy dose of normality was just what he needed after the past twenty-four hours.

Mrs Grigor, the old woman who lived across the road, was at her window when Denzel passed. He gave her a wave and was a little surprised when she didn't wave back. Mind you, her eyes weren't what they used to be, and she wouldn't have been expecting to see Denzel passing so early in the afternoon.

Denzel whistled as he strolled up the path, bouncing a finger along the top of the fence beside it. When he reached the door he fumbled in his pocket for his key, then looked up when the front door opened. Owen, the younger of his dads, stood in the doorway, still dressed in his short-sleeved work shirt and tie. To Denzel's relief, he was smiling. It looked like Quinn had provided him with a convincing story, just as she'd promised.

"Hi there!" said Owen. "Spotted you coming up the path, thought I'd beat you to it!"

"Yeah, sorry about last night," said Denzel. He moved

to duck past, but Owen quickly placed a hand on the doorframe, blocking the way.

"Uh… Last night?" Owen said.

"Yeah," said Denzel. "You know, not being here."

Owen nodded slowly. "Right. Yeah. Gotcha," he said. "So… How can I help you?"

Denzel blinked. "Well, you could start by letting me in."

Owen looked him up and down. "Uh, and why would I do that?"

"Because I live here," said Denzel.

A range of expressions crossed Owen's face, like it couldn't figure out which one it should be aiming for. It finally settled on something that was equal parts amusement and confusion. "Sorry, I think you must have the wrong house."

The fine hairs on the back of Denzel's neck tingled. He tried to speak, but on the first attempt the words snagged at the back of his throat.

"Very funny, Owen. Now, come on, let me in," he eventually managed. He tried to squeeze through the gap between his dad and the doorframe. Owen quickly moved his body to block the space.

"What are you…? Stop it," Owen said. "You're not coming in. You've got the wrong house."

SPECTRE COLLECTORS

"Owen, it's me! Stop messing around," Denzel said. "Let me in!" he demanded, trying to force his way into the hall.

"Jack! Jack!" Owen cried, gripping the doorframe and shoving Denzel back with his hip. "Home invader! Home invader!"

There was a thudding from the stairs as Jack, the older of Denzel's adoptive parents, took them two at a time. His shirt and tie covered his top half, but on his bottom half he wore his gym shorts and battered old running shoes.

"What's the matter?" Jack demanded. "What's going on?"

"It's this kid," said Owen, frantically trying to shove Denzel back out into the garden. "He's trying to get in."

"All right, easy, easy," Jack said, taking hold of Owen's arm and guiding him aside. Denzel stumbled through into the hall, only to find the much larger Jack blocking the way. "Are you OK, son?" Jack asked.

Denzel felt a surge of hope. "You know me?" he said. "Tell me you recognise me."

Jack smiled and put a hand on Denzel's shoulder. Denzel let out a big pent-up breath of relief. "You do. You recognise me," he said. Jack gave his shoulder a comforting squeeze.

"I'm sorry, son," he said softly. "I've never seen you before in my life."

The world spun. The doormat beneath Denzel's feet seemed to turn to quicksand, pulling him down. His heart raced. His stomach tightened. He began to tremble as hot tears filled his eyes. "No. No, it's me. It's me. You can't have forgotten. You can't have!"

Jack crouched down, keeping the hand on Denzel's shoulder. "Hey. Hey, it's OK," he soothed. "Don't get upset. Do you want us to call your parents?"

"You *are* my parents!" Denzel cried. Owen and Jack looked at each other in surprise, and Denzel saw his chance. With a shove, he knocked Jack off balance and raced for the stairs. He scrambled up them on his hands and knees, his pulse pounding, his back slick with panic-sweat.

He could already hear footsteps behind him as he reached the top, but his bedroom door was dead ahead now. He hurried for it, throwing it open and diving inside.

Denzel stopped.

He sunk to the floor, and his knees thudded against the bare wooden floorboards. He could hear Jack's voice, sterner now, but his heart was crashing too loudly in his ears for him to be able to make out the words.

His room was empty. The bed was gone. The walls

were bare. He couldn't even see the pinholes where his posters had been, let alone the posters themselves. It was as if he had never been there at all.

"My room," Denzel said, and the words echoed strangely in the empty space. "They took my room."

Jack was still talking, but it was Owen's voice that Denzel heard. "I'm calling the police."

Denzel stood and turned. "What? No. Owen, no. Don't. Please. Why would the room be empty? Why do you have a completely empty room inside your house, if it isn't mine?"

Owen opened his mouth to reply, but a frown flitted across his brow. He glanced across the bare walls. "Because ... we haven't got around to decorating," Owen said.

"Look, you're not in trouble, son," said Jack. "But you're upset. We need to find your parents."

Denzel looked at them both for a long time. He knew their faces better than he knew his own, but he felt the need to commit every line, every detail to memory. Finally, he wiped his eyes on his sleeve. "They won't find them," he said, his voice cracking. "They're gone."

He clenched his fists and gritted his teeth. "But I swear, I'm going to get them back."

Denzel ran, leaving his bedroom, his house and his dads behind. His eyes blurred with tears again as he looked back to see Jack closing the front door. He kept watching the house for as long as he—

WHAM! Denzel crashed into something hard and metallic. He bounced off and landed on his bum. He looked up at the white van he'd run into the side of. From inside, he could just make out a frantic muttering.

Jumping up, Denzel banged his fist against the van's sliding door. "Boyle! Samara! Open up, I know you're in there!" Denzel shouted. The door stayed closed, so Denzel spun away from the van and cupped his hands around his mouth. "Secret ghost-hunting society! Come and see the secret ghost-hunting society! Hiding in this van!"

The door opened. A hand caught Denzel by the back of his school jumper and yanked him inside. "Shut up," Boyle hissed, as the door slid closed again. "What do you think you're doing?"

"Change them back," said Denzel. "Change them back. Now."

Boyle and Samara exchanged a glance. "Change who back?" Samara asked.

"My parents. My dads. Change them back!"

"Back to what? What have they been changed into?

What are you talking about?" Boyle barked.

"They've forgotten me," Denzel said. "You did that thing you do, and they've forgotten me!"

Samara's hand went to her mouth. Even Boyle blinked in surprise. Denzel looked between them both, his head flicking back and forth like a spectator at a tennis match. "It wasn't you," he realised. "You didn't do it, did you?"

"No," Samara said. "No. I'm sorry. It wasn't us. It must've been Director Quinn."

"That's enough, Samara," Boyle said.

"She must have sent someone. Knightley and Rasmus, maybe, to—"

"I said that's enough!" said Boyle, raising his voice.

"It doesn't matter who did it," Denzel said. He rounded on Samara, taking her hands in his and squeezing them tightly. "You can fix them, right? You can make them remember?"

Samara cleared her throat. "I'm sorry, Denzel," she said. "There's nothing I can do. Once their memory has been wiped, there's no way of putting it back."

"You mean ... they've really forgotten me?" said Denzel.

"Yes," said Samara softly. "They've forgotten you, Denzel. Forever."

CHAPTER 14

Denzel sprinted along the corridor, leaving Samara and Boyle trailing behind. When he reached the doors to Quinn's office he raised a fist to hammer against them, but the doors swung inward before he could connect.

"Ah, Denzel, you came back," said Quinn. She was sitting on a high-backed leather chair beside a small table. "Tea?" she asked, holding up a delicate china teapot.

Denzel hurried into the room, and the doors swung closed behind him before Boyle and Samara could catch up. "You wiped their memories," he said. "You stole my parents!"

SPECTRE COLLECTORS

"A rather dramatic way of putting it," said Quinn. She gestured to the chair opposite her. "Please, sit down. Let's discuss it like grown-ups."

"*Discuss* it? There's nothing to discuss," said Denzel. "You used that magic powder stuff and you wiped me from their heads." He dug his fingernails into his palms to stop his voice cracking. "And you're going to put me back."

Quinn raised a cup of tea to her lips and blew gently on it. "First of all, there was no 'magic powder stuff' involved. That would have been utterly impractical. If we used that on your parents, then what about your neighbours? Your school? They'd still remember. We've tried that approach with others before, but it's always an administrative nightmare. You can't begin to imagine the paperwork."

She took a sip of her tea, then set the cup back down in her saucer. "Luckily, I devised a much simpler method a few years ago. Picture your life like a thread, Denzel. A shining golden thread that weaves through the world, finding an anchor point in the minds of each and every person you've ever met. It criss-crosses, left, right, up, down, hopping cities and counties and countries, spreading the knowledge of your existence throughout the Earth. A shining web, with you at the centre."

She took a sugar cube from the bowl, popped it in her mouth, then crunched it. "Removing all those anchor points would be impossible," she said. "But pull the thread…" She mimed doing just that. "And the whole web unravels."

Denzel shifted on the balls of his feet. "What do you mean? What have you done?"

"I mean it isn't just your parents who have forgotten you, Denzel. Everyone has. Everyone who isn't a Spectre Collector, at least. Your life was a stitch in time. I have unpicked that stitch. It's like you have never even existed. Your parents don't remember you, Denzel, because to all intents and purposes, there was never anything for them to forget."

"But … Smithy. He remembered me."

Quinn raised an eyebrow then shook her head. "Not any more."

"No!" cried Denzel. "No, that's not true. You're lying."

Quinn raised a hand, fingers splayed, then snatched at the air. An invisible force grabbed Denzel by the front of his school jumper and dragged him across the floor. He gasped as he was forcibly slammed into the chair, knocking the wind from him.

The director leaned in closer and stared deep into Denzel's eyes. He felt a dull ache behind his eyeballs, and as Quinn's stare intensified, the ache crawled all the way upwards into his brain.

"Now, Denzel, as I said yesterday, I believe you could be a useful addition to our ranks," Quinn purred, and Denzel felt his arms and legs become too heavy for him to move. "So what say you and I have a little chat about your future?"

Denzel lay on his back on his uncomfortable bed again, gazing up at the ceiling, and trying to think about the world beyond. A world which had completely forgotten he'd ever been part of it.

Of course, that was for the best. Quinn had explained it and made him see that the work of the Spectre Collectors was important, and that he had a vital role to play in it. People's lives depended on it. The safety of the whole world depended on it.

And yet...

He thought that maybe, just maybe, he missed his dads. Quinn had told him not to, and for a while, at least, his brain had obeyed. He remembered them, of course, but Quinn had instructed him not to miss them, and the sense of longing and loss he felt had quickly faded like shadows in the morning sun.

Now, though, lying in his room in the half-dark, he

could feel it stirring again. Everything the director had said had made sense at the time. Now he was alone, her words were twisting around so he couldn't quite remember why he had been so convinced by them.

And yet, it was for the best. It was all for the best.

His head spun and his breath came in short gulps. Quinn had done something to him, he knew. He hadn't minded at the time. He'd welcomed her taking his pain and sadness away, in fact. But now...

But now...

Whatever he was feeling, it wasn't pleasant. He closed his eyes, hoping it would pass as quickly as it had arrived. He tried to calm his breathing. Quinn's voice rolled like a marble inside his head, telling him not to worry, not to be afraid, not to get upset.

"Yes," he mumbled. "It's for the best..."

"*Denzel!*"

"Wha—"

Denzel opened one eye and swivelled it around, trying to make sense of where he was and what was happening. Samara stood just inside the door, looking down at him. His vision was blurry and there was a string of drool dangling from his lips.

"Did I wake you?" Samara whispered.

Denzel forced his other eye to open, then stretched.

"What? No. No, I was awake," he said. He yawned. "What time is it?"

"Just after 3am," Samara said.

"In the morning?"

"That's generally what the 'am' bit means, yeah," Samara said. She bit her lip. "Are you OK?"

Denzel swung his legs down off the bed and yawned again. "Yeah. Why?"

"Not upset about your parents or anything?" Samara pressed.

Denzel shook his head slowly. His brow furrowed. "Uh... No. Not... I mean..." He cleared his throat. "No. I'm fine. It's... It's for the best."

Samara glanced back at the door, then knelt down in front of Denzel. "That's Quinn talking, not you. She did something to you so you'd stop being angry at her and join us. She messed with your head." She looked deep into his eyes. "Do you trust me, Denzel?"

After a moment, Denzel nodded. "I think so, yeah."

"Good," said Samara. "I think Quinn is up to something. I've had suspicions for a while, and what she did to you and your dads has got me even more worried."

She glanced back at the door, as if worried someone might be listening there. "You said something about her having a plan. Do you know what she meant?"

"No," said Denzel, shaking his head. "Just... Just that she said it would get rid of the ghosts. Once and for all."

"But that's impossible," Samara whispered. "How could she do that?"

"There's something else, too," said Denzel. "I didn't tell anyone because, well, I didn't know what to do."

"What is it?" asked Samara.

"The poltergeist. It … spoke to me."

Samara's eyes widened. "Spoke to you?"

"Yes. Well, no. Well, sort of," said Denzel. "It spelled out a message. You know, with its arms or legs or whatever they are."

"What did it say?"

"It said 'help us'," Denzel told her.

Samara blinked in surprise. "*Help us*?" she said. "Help who? The ghosts?"

"I don't know," said Denzel. "I thought you might."

"No idea," Samara admitted.

Denzel looked up at the ceiling for a moment as he steadied his nerve, then back at Samara. "Then maybe we should go and find out?"

Denzel glanced nervously back into the corridor as Samara closed the door of a room marked *Spectral Storage 4*. His eyes darted to a CCTV camera mounted near the ceiling.

"You sure no one will have seen us?" he whispered.

"Positive," said Samara. She held up her wrist, revealing a watch-like device with a red light blinking on it. "Signal jammer. I stole it from Boyle earlier and programmed it to loop the feeds. Anyone watching will just see an empty room."

"I thought tech stuff was Boyle's department," said Denzel.

Samara shrugged. "I like to dabble."

The room was several metres long, with rows and rows of metal boxes lining the walls. Samara brushed her fingertips across a few of them, and sparkles danced in the air at her touch.

"And it *definitely* said 'help us'?" she asked.

Denzel nodded. "With its tentacle things," he said. "I thought it was attacking me, but it wasn't. It was asking for help."

"If that's true then maybe that's why it came to you in the first place," Samara said. "Maybe that's why you could see it. Come to think of it, the Freeform – the bin-monster – it didn't actually attack you, either. Normally something like that would've torn you in half, or ripped your head off, or eaten your—"

"All right, all right! I get the picture," said Denzel.

Samara chewed her lip. "What if they both came to you for help?"

"But why ask me?" said Denzel. "What can I do?"

Samara stopped at one of the boxes, then backtracked to the one before it. "This is it," she said. She shot Denzel a worried look. "But I'm really not sure about this."

Denzel half-smiled. "Do you trust me, Samara?"

After a moment, Samara nodded. "I think so, yeah."

Denzel winced. "Just so you know, I was sort of hoping you'd say 'no' there, and I could go back to bed and forget this whole thing." He took a deep breath. "But let's do it. I mean, what's the worst that could happen, right?"

Samara opened her mouth, but Denzel quickly stopped her. "Please don't answer that question."

"OK," said Samara. "Here goes."

She pressed her hand against the front of the box and muttered something below her breath. There was a loud *hiss*, like steam escaping, and the box slid smoothly forwards until it was sticking several centimetres out of the wall.

They peered inside and saw a red gem wrapped in thin willow branches. Samara unwound the branches, then stepped back and stood by Denzel. "Anything?" she whispered.

"No," began Denzel, but then he saw it – a tiny curl of

black smoke snaking up out of the box like the tentacle of a baby octopus. "Wait, yes, I see it. It's coming out," Denzel said.

He took a shuffled step closer to the box. "Hey, it's OK. Don't worry. We won't hurt you," he soothed, then he jumped back and screamed as the smoke exploded out of the box.

It flew upwards like a startled octopus, slamming its long tentacles against the ceiling. Samara clamped her hand over Denzel's mouth and followed his gaze. "Where is it? Up there?"

Denzel nodded. The poltergeist pulsated and squirmed, as if getting ready to attack. Pulling Samara's hand away, Denzel swallowed nervously. "It's OK," he said, raising his hands to try to calm the ghostly shape. "You said you needed help. That's why we're here."

The 'geist shifted from side to side on the ceiling, as if drifting on the wind. Its pulsating slowed, just a little. "But I can't help you unless you tell me what's wrong," Denzel said. He smiled hopefully. "So, uh, fancy a chat?"

The poltergeist lunged. The tips of its tentacles all came together to form a point – a point which, to Denzel's dismay, was right in the middle of his head. He felt a sensation of icy cold flood through him, like his blood was turning to liquid nitrogen in his veins. He opened his mouth to scream again, but all that rolled out was a gasp of frosty white air and a somewhat muted, "Ow."

Images began flickering through Denzel's head, like the pages of a flipbook being turned at super speed. He saw faces and places he didn't recognise, heard voices shouting to him in languages he couldn't understand. Eyes, teeth, doors, rooms – his brain went numb as thousands of pictures and sounds and sensations all flooded his senses at once.

And then it stopped. Everything stopped.

He was looking down on an empty white space. At first, he thought he was alone, but then he felt them beside him, supporting him, and there was a rush of relief that swept all the way up from his toes.

"Keep watching, Denzel," his dads whispered, each taking one of his hands and squeezing it. "This is important."

As they spoke, the whiteness thinned like a mist, revealing shapes lurking within. He saw himself, stumbling along a dimly lit corridor, clutching his stomach and doing the walk he knew he only did when he was desperate for a wee.

"I don't remember this," he said.

The dream-Denzel – because this felt like a dream – looked relieved when he found a bathroom and stumbled inside. There was a flash as time leapt forwards, and a much less stressed Denzel emerged into the corridor.

Both Denzels gasped at the sight of Knightley and Rasmus. They were moving along the hallway, a third figure held between them. It wasn't until they drew closer that Denzel recognised the old woman from the supermarket. Her head was back to normal, and she made a grab for Denzel as she got close.

"Help me! You don't know what she'll do. You don't know what she'll do!"

The dream-Denzel started to ask Knightley and Rasmus what she was talking about, but then Rasmus was opening a bag and blowing, and a swirl of dust fluttered up into Denzel's nostrils, and filled his head with light.

Denzel's body convulsed violently. A hand caught him – the *real* him – by the arm. He heard Samara calling to him and the light began to fade. "N-no," he stammered. "Not yet."

More pictures flashed before his eyes, even faster this time. He saw gems – hundreds of gems – smashed to pieces. He saw Quinn opening a box. It was the one he'd picked up at the armoury, he thought. The one Boyle said had been stolen.

He saw her standing with her arms aloft, her body encased in an eerie electric glow.

He saw a rip in the world, bright and swirling with colour. He saw reality turn itself inside out. He saw chaos and death and destruction.

And then he saw nothing but darkness.

In the dark, Denzel reached for his dads' hands, but they were no longer there. They were gone. Taken from him.

The ache Denzel had felt behind his eyes since his confrontation with Quinn fizzled then faded away. Denzel blinked, and he was back in the room with Samara and the poltergeist, which was pulsing gently on the ceiling.

He stumbled sideways into Samara's arms. "Are you OK?" she asked. "What happened?"

Denzel took a series of deep breaths, trying to steady his nerves and stop himself vomiting all over Samara's neatly pressed robe. "Doesn't matter what happened," he managed. "It's what's *about* to happen that we need to worry about."

CHAPTER 15

Convincing the poltergeist it had to go back into the box wasn't easy, but after around twenty minutes of pleading, promises and persuasion, it reluctantly squeezed itself back inside.

Over the next hour and a half, Denzel and Samara sat on Denzel's bed while Denzel did his best to explain everything he'd seen and heard. The fact that Denzel didn't really know what he'd seen and heard made this quite tricky.

From what he could piece together, he'd got up to go to the toilet the night after the supermarket encounter, spotted Knightley and Rasmus with the old woman, then after she'd tried to ask Denzel for help, Rasmus had wiped his memory.

Beyond that … he wasn't sure. He didn't know what the stuff with Quinn and the big hole in the world was telling him.

What he did know was that he was angry. Quinn had wiped him from his parents' minds, and then did something to his head that had somehow made him not care. Whatever she'd done had worn off when the poltergeist had stuck its tentacles into his brain though, and Denzel was now itching to face Quinn down.

"So…" said Samara, drawing the word out until it had at least two syllables. "She's going to put a hole in the world?"

"Right," Denzel said. "I mean, I think so. That's what it looked like."

Samara shrugged. "We do that a lot. I did it at the supermarket, remember? It's a short cut. It sort of folds space so you can hop from one spot to another."

Denzel shook his head. "No, it wasn't like that. It was … colourful. Inside. There were shapes moving. Sort of swirling around."

Samara raised her eyebrows. "That sounds like the Spectral Realm. Why would she be opening the Spectral Realm? That's… Well, I mean, it's insanely dangerous, for a start. There are so many rules against it, there's no way she'd even try."

"Well, she's going to," said Denzel.

"Assuming we can trust a poltergeist who implanted a vision into your head."

"Hey, if you can't trust one of them, who *can* you trust?" said Denzel.

Samara smiled. "Yeah, it'd still be good to know for sure, though. We can't really confront her with 'A ghost told us you're up to something'. We need more."

"You said you had suspicions already," Denzel reminded her.

"Yeah, but just that. Suspicions. Not evidence."

Denzel thought for a moment. "Maybe Boyle could help."

"No," said Samara. "No. Boyle's a good guy, but boy, he loves his rules and regs. If he finds out we've been sneaking about... No. Not a good idea."

She glanced down at the device on her wrist and stood up. "Speaking of Boyle, though, I'd better get this back to his locker before he starts looking for it." Samara paused with her hand on the door handle. "You'll be OK for now? Don't go confronting Quinn. Not yet."

Denzel nodded. "I know."

"OK, then." Samara smiled. "It's all going to be fine,"

she said, then she turned the handle, opened the door and let out a gasp.

Boyle stood right outside, like he'd been lurking out there just waiting for the door to open. Samara looked him up and down, pausing just briefly on the rifle he held in both hands.

"Uh, hey, partner," Samara said. "I was just checking in on our new recruit."

Denzel stood up and appeared at Samara's back. "Boyle. Hey. How you doing? Ready for some more training?"

Boyle's eyes narrowed. "Director Quinn wants to see you both," he said.

Samara and Denzel exchanged a glance. "Us?" Samara began. "Why does she—"

"Now," Boyle said. He pivoted on one foot and nodded along the corridor in the direction of Quinn's office. He held his hand out to Samara, palm open. "And I'd like my scrambler back."

Quinn was writing at her desk when Boyle marched Denzel and Samara in to see her. She didn't look up until the door closed with a soft *click* that somehow managed to sound deafening in the hush of the office.

For a long time, the director didn't speak. Instead, she

just tick-tocked her gaze slowly between Samara and Denzel, like she was trying to decide which one to shout at first.

At last, her gaze settled on Samara. "Well," Quinn said. "I'm very disappointed."

"I know, I know," said Samara. "We should've done more magic training by now. It's my fault, I've been—"

Quinn twitched. "Stop," she said in a tone so cold Denzel could have sworn the temperature actually dropped a degree. "You took Boyle's scrambler. You went to Spectral Storage. Why?"

Samara tried to smile, but it was fooling no one. "Just some extra training," she said. "That's all."

"Tell the truth, Samara," Boyle snapped. "You're only making it worse."

"It wasn't her, it was me," Denzel said. "It was my idea."

Director Quinn's eyes crept across to him. "Was it really?"

"We know what you're up to," Denzel said. "We know what you're planning. We know everything."

"Do you?" asked Quinn, raising an eyebrow. "Do tell."

Denzel sniffed. "What?"

"You know what I'm planning." Quinn placed her elbows on her desk and leaned forwards on them. "Do enlighten me."

Denzel cleared his throat. "Well… You took that thing from the armoury. The disruptor thing."

"The Spectral Disruptor. Yes. And?" Quinn asked. "I regularly make modifications to our equipment. That's no secret."

Quinn caught the expression of surprise on Denzel's face and laughed. It was a dry scrape at the back of her throat that set Denzel's teeth on edge.

"The old woman. The Corporeal. You said she got away, but she didn't. Knightley and Rasmus had her. Last night."

Quinn's laughter died in her throat. Her eyes darted to Boyle and Samara, just for a moment, then settled back on Denzel again. "I'm afraid you are mistaken, Denzel."

"No! I'm not," Denzel continued. "She's here! She asked for my help, and so did the poltergeist. They're afraid. Of you. Of what you're planning to do!"

Quinn steepled her fingers in front of her. "And what, pray tell, am I planning to do?"

Denzel ran out of steam at that point. "I don't know," he admitted.

"Ha. As I thought," said Quinn. "That's because I'm not planning to do—"

"But I know it involves opening the Spectre Realm!"

said Denzel.

"Spectral Realm," Samara corrected.

"Sorry. Spectral Realm."

"Don't be ridiculous," Boyle grunted.

Quinn's not-quite smile became a not-at-all smile. "Who have you been speaking to?" she asked, then she waved a hand. "Doesn't matter."

She tapped a finger on her desktop for several seconds, looking Denzel up and down. "Do you know how many ghosts there are in the world, Denzel?"

Denzel shook his head. "No."

Quinn nodded slowly, then turned to the others. "Samara? Boyle? Would you like to tell him?"

"Uh, we don't know," said Samara. "No one does."

"It's impossible to know," Boyle added.

"Precisely!" said Quinn. "We have no idea. We've never had any idea. And yet we go out there, day in, day out, catching them, putting them away, catching them, putting them away. The same thing, over and over and over again, like we're stuck in a loop.

"Do you know how many lives have been lost thanks to this never-ending battle of ours?" Quinn continued. She pointed towards the ceiling. "Not just them up there, but us. Down *here*. My life. Yours. The lives of thousands of children who never got to have a childhood."

She inhaled so deeply through her nose Denzel felt like she was sucking all the air out of the room. "And for what? What difference have we made? There are still ghosts. There are still creatures lurking in the shadows and monsters under the bed. Ten thousand lost children, and we have achieved precisely nothing."

"We've saved people," said Samara.

"And for what? What thanks do we get?" Quinn demanded. "And have you seen *people*?" she asked, spitting the word out. "Most of them don't deserve saving."

"What are you going to do?" Samara asked.

"I'm going to free us. All of us," Quinn said. "And you're going to help me, Denzel."

"Me? How?"

"I'm going to need you to tell me if we've got them all," Quinn said.

"Got all what?" asked Denzel.

"The ghosts. You're going to make sure there are none of them left after I open the Spectral Realm and suck them all inside."

Samara let out a gasp. "What? You can't do that!"

"I can, and I will," said Quinn. "I've been able to recalibrate the Spectral Disruptor to open a doorway. All those ghosts who are stuck on this side? They'll all be sent to where they belong, whether they like it or not. No more hauntings. No more disturbances. No more *ghosts*."

Denzel felt Samara stiffen beside him. "But ... we can't just interfere in the Spectral Realm. It's far too dangerous. It goes against everything we're supposed to stand for."

"With all due respect, director, it's against the rules," said Boyle.

"With all due respect, Boyle, if I wanted your opinion I'd ask for it," Quinn spat. "I'm director. I set the rules."

"You're only director of this chapter," Samara said. "The Elders wouldn't approve of this. I want to talk to them."

"Do you? Do you really?" Quinn sighed. She thrust a hand towards Samara. Samara opened her mouth to speak, but all that emerged was a faint croak. "Let's see you talk to them now," Quinn told her.

"You don't want to do this. I've seen what happens. You'll destroy the world!" Denzel demanded.

"Nonsense. I will *save* it," said Quinn.

"No! I've seen it, and you won't!" Denzel insisted. "What about the old woman with the octopus head? And the broken gems I saw. What are they for?"

Quinn looked a little taken aback again. She smiled thinly. "You are full of surprises, young man. The gems act as ... a battery, let's say, for the disruptor. Without them, the machine can't access the necessary frequency to open the doorway. And, as for the Corporeal ... I dissected it. The knowledge I gained from it proved most invaluable."

"That's why they're afraid," Denzel realised. "You're hurting them."

"Ridiculous," Quinn said. "They're not alive. They don't feel anything."

"They do!" Denzel insisted. "And they're terrified of your machine. It hurts them. Or ... they're scared it's going to hurt them, or something."

"Enough of this nonsense. Of course it doesn't *hurt* them or *scare* them. They feel *nothing*," Quinn said. "Boyle, get them both out of my sight. Lock them up. I'll deal with them later."

Boyle adjusted his grip on his gun. He swung the barrel in Denzel's direction, but hesitated. Samara looked at him imploringly. She tried to speak, but her voice was barely even a whisper.

"What if he's right?" Boyle said. "What if they do feel?"

"They don't," Quinn said.

"But what if they do?"

Quinn's face flared purple. "*So what if they do?*" she roared, and her voice shook several of her books from their shelves. "Hmm? So what if they do feel? So what if it does hurt? They're creatures. Things. No, they're less than that. They're *nothing*."

A wind whipped up around her like a mini-tornado. She curved her fingers into claws, and snakes of energy crackled in the spaces between them. "Now, do as you are told, like a good little soldier, and get them out of my sight!" she hissed.

Boyle looked pained as he turned the gun on his partner. "I'm sorry, Samara," he whispered.

"Boyle, don't," Samara pleaded.

"I'm afraid I'm going to have to ask you to *duck*."

Samara blinked. Her eyes went wide. She dropped on to her front just as Boyle squeezed the trigger. Denzel felt a movement in the air beside him. He heard Quinn cry out in surprise, then turned in time to see her sliding backwards across the floor. She leaned forwards, one arm out in front of her like a rugby player racing for a try. The other arm drew back, a ball of blue fire forming in her palm.

Samara coughed as her voice returned. "Look out," she warned, sweeping her hands in front of her just as Quinn let fly with the fireball. A patch of air shimmered, then went solid. The fireball exploded against it, and the shield was quickly consumed by the blue flames.

Boyle adjusted a lever on the side of his rifle, then took aim again. He squeezed the trigger and a long, thin beam of white energy shot from the barrel like water from a fire hose.

Quinn raised a hand and the beam stopped half a metre ahead of her. The electrical glow cast flickering shadow across her face, wrapping her features in ominous darkness. She regarded the beam with something like amusement, then began conjuring another fireball in her other hand.

"Brace yourselves!" Samara warned.

Denzel looked at Quinn. He looked at Boyle. Lunging forwards, he grabbed Boyle's gun and jerked it upwards. The beam cut a trench up the back wall and across the ceiling, before hitting the chandelier directly above Quinn's head in a shower of sparks and shattering crystal.

The director looked up just as the chandelier dropped down. She raised her hands, but too late. The floor shook as the enormous ornate light fitting smashed down on top of her.

The echo bounced around the office, then faded until the only sound was the rasping of Denzel's panicky breathing. Boyle gave Denzel a curt nod. "Good call with the chandelier."

"Thanks," Denzel panted. "What do we do now?"

SPECTRE COLLECTORS

In the middle of the room, the chandelier vibrated, then began to rise into the air. Samara caught Denzel by the arm. "Now," she said, "we run!"

CHAPTER 16

Denzel stood at the back of the lift, where he'd been forcibly shoved by both Samara and Boyle in turn. Samara knelt just inside the door, hands raised, ready to unleash some serious magic on anyone unlucky enough to be waiting on the other side of it. Boyle was behind her, the butt of his rifle pressed against his shoulder, his sights trained on the door as the lift sped towards the surface.

"Why don't we just tell everyone what she's up to?" Denzel asked. "You said messing with the spirit world or whatever was against the rules, right?"

"Right," said Boyle. "But we've got no proof. Everyone

would take her side."

"And even if they did believe us, Quinn's a twelfth-level Oberon. There's no saying we'd be able to stop her," Samara added. "Even all together."

"So we just run away and leave her to it?" Denzel asked.

"We make a tactical withdrawal," Boyle said. "And get backup."

"We can try to contact the Elders," Samara said.

"Right. Fair enough, then," said Denzel. "Who are the Elders when they're at home?"

"They founded the Spectre Collectors," Boyle explained.

Denzel frowned. "Didn't you say it was hundreds of years old?"

"Yes," said Samara. "Yes, I did." Before she could say any more, the lift jerked to a sudden stop.

"That can't be good," Denzel muttered, struggling to keep his balance.

"They're on to us," Boyle said. He smashed the stock of his rifle against the metal covering surrounding the lift's only two buttons. At once, the lift began to plunge downwards.

"Wah!" Denzel yelped, clinging to the walls as the sudden g-force shoved his cheeks up into his eyes. "What did you do that for?"

Boyle swung again, slamming the butt of the weapon against the metal covering. A corner buckled and he dug his fingers underneath. "Wasn't me," Boyle said. "Trying to fix it."

"Hurry!" Samara urged, raising her voice above the sound of the air whistling around the lift as it streaked downwards.

"Can't you magic it or something?" asked Denzel.

"'*Magic it*'? No, I can't 'magic it'. It's protected against hexes."

"But it's going to stop at the bottom, right?"

"Definitely going to stop at the bottom," Boyle said. "Very abruptly and with a spectacular amount of damage."

Denzel swallowed. "Oh. Great."

Boyle yanked on the metal plate, tearing it free and revealing a spaghetti of electrical wires. He plunged his hands inside and began pulling connectors apart.

"Getting near the bottom," Samara warned.

"Almost ... got it," Boyle said, frantically disconnecting and reconnecting the wiring. "There!" he announced.

Denzel and Samara shot upwards and slammed against the ceiling as the lift accelerated rapidly. Down, down, down it plummeted, picking up speed as it raced towards the floor of the shaft somewhere not too far below.

Boyle clung to a clump of wiring, his legs flapping up somewhere around the ceiling. "W-wait," he grimaced. "Red wire, not blue."

"Hurry!" Samara cried.

Boyle twisted two wires together. Denzel and Samara slammed against the floor as the lift screeched to a stop, then started back upwards again.

"This can't be good for you," Denzel wheezed, as the increase in gravity pressed him against the floor. "I feel like a pancake."

"We could always try the alternative," Boyle grimaced.

"What's that?" asked Denzel.

"Smashing into the ground at high speed," Boyle said.

Denzel gritted his teeth. "Let's stick with this for now."

Fighting against the g-force, Boyle reached back into the tangle of wires and fiddled with a few connections. The lift slowed enough that they were all able to stand up.

"When we stop, stick close to us," Samara told Denzel.

"No worries on that front," said Denzel. "You're the ones with the guns and magic and all that."

"Yeah, but everyone who'll be coming after us has those, too," Boyle pointed out. "We'll have to move fast."

Denzel glanced around them. "Can't we just disable the lift so they can't get up?"

"Do you really think we've only got one lift?" Boyle said, scowling. "Billions of pounds of technology down there, and you think there's only one way in and out?"

He pressed his rifle to his shoulder and took aim at the door again. "Fact is, they're probably already up there. This might just be the shortest escape attempt in history."

The lift lurched to a shuddering stop. Samara and Boyle took their positions, hands and gun raised. "Stay back, Denzel," Samara whispered.

"Way ahead of you," said Denzel, ducking behind Boyle.

Samara beckoned with one finger and the door swung inwards, revealing empty space beyond. Boyle pressed a button on the side of his gun and leaned forward, sweeping the barrel across the entrance of the lift.

"Picking anything up?" Samara asked.

"No," said Boyle. "You?"

Samara shook her head. "Clear, I think. Let's go."

Boyle and Samara stepped out of the lift and scanned the area around them. The alleyway behind the church was clear. "Come on," Samara urged, and Denzel hurried out of the lift to join them.

At the corner of the church, Boyle made an elaborate hand movement that Denzel guessed was either a signal to stay back, or an extremely rude gesture. Boyle spent several seconds scanning with his gun, and glancing around at anything someone might feasibly be hiding behind.

"It's too quiet," he whispered. "It looks too safe."

"Can it ever really be *too* safe?" Denzel asked.

"Too safe usually means it isn't safe at all," Samara said. She reached into the folds of her robe and pulled out what looked like a toy version of the van she and Boyle had been driving earlier.

Taking aim, she tossed the toy underarm out into the car park. It bounced once on the tarmac, then landed on its wheels. Samara mumbled below her breath. There was a sound like two balloons rubbing together, and where the toy had stood was now a full-sized van.

"What are you doing?" Boyle hissed. "They'll follow."

Samara nodded. "That's the idea," she said. She waved her hand and the van's engine started up. With a screeching of tyres, it raced out of the car park and skidded on to the road.

Denzel watched the van drive off. "Should we... Aren't we meant to be in that?" he asked, but Samara pressed a finger to her lips.

There was a *thud* as the front doors of the church were thrown wide. Half a dozen silver and blue motorbikes roared out from within, a Vulteron leaning low in the saddle of each one. They pulled wheelies across the car park, then banked on to the road and set off in pursuit of the van. Samara looked pleased with herself as she watched them speed away.

"Ah, the magically-controlled-decoy-van technique," she said, leading the others out from their hiding place behind the church. "Oldest trick in the book."

A blast of energy punched a basketball-sized hole in the wall just ahead of her. Boyle turned, snapping up his gun. "Don't!" Knightley warned. She stepped out from behind a parked car, a scary-looking handgun in each hand. One of the guns was trained on Samara, the other on Boyle. Denzel was quite pleased to find he'd been left out.

"Drop your piece, Boyle," Knightley instructed. She shot Samara a sideways glance. "Keep your hands where I can see them, and don't even think about twiddling those fingers, Princess."

There was a rippling in the air behind her. A hook-nosed figure in an Oberon robe stepped out of empty space, dusted himself down, then pointed his hands vaguely in the direction of Denzel and the others.

"Rasmus," Samara said, spitting the word out as if it left a nasty taste. "Knew you wouldn't be far away."

"Samara," said Rasmus, drawing out the S like a snake. "You've really managed to get yourself in trouble this time."

"Enough with the chit-chat," Knightley said. "Drop your weapon, Boyle. I won't tell you again."

"You're not going to shoot us, Knightley," Boyle said.

Knightley's eyes narrowed. "Is that right?"

She pulled the trigger. Denzel saw something blue streaking towards Boyle. Boyle raised his forearm and a semi-transparent shield flicked up in front of him, deflecting the energy bolt towards the sky.

Knightley opened fire with the other gun. Samara ducked and part of the wall behind her exploded into the church. She clapped her hands together and something that looked like a tidal wave of wind raced towards Knightley and Rasmus.

Rasmus raised both hands and the air turned to crystal in front of them, deflecting the wind-wave.

"Take cover in the church," Boyle growled, raining laser-fire on the crystal shield.

Denzel hopped from foot to foot. "Shouldn't I, you know, help you guys?"

Samara and Boyle both shot him a withering glance.

Denzel smiled weakly. "Fair point. I'll hide in the church."

Ducking through the hole that Knightley had blasted, Denzel scrambled over a mound of fallen rubble. He slid up and over a big chunk of masonry, then looked around for a place to hide.

The layout of the church was confusingly un-church-like. He'd expected a big room with lots of wooden benches and an equally wooden Jesus at the far end. Instead, he was in a long corridor with doors leading off from both sides. He hurried along it, realising that the church wasn't actually a church at all, but part of the Spectre Collector HQ buried deep below.

A side branch ran off from the main corridor. Denzel glanced back at the hole in the wall. Colourful lights flickered and flashed. Stuff went *fzzt, brrrm* and *wssssht*, though not necessarily in that order. Something exploded, imploded, then exploded all over again. Even from Denzel's limited point of view, the battle outside looked like the Lifetime Achievement Award showreel of a Hollywood special effects artist.

Denzel ducked down the side corridor. There were another two doors standing directly across from each other, but he didn't know what lurked beyond them, so decided it was safer not to chance it.

At the end of the corridor, just before it stopped at a

solid wall, was a little alcove. It wasn't very deep, but it was just big enough for him to tuck himself inside. He squashed himself against the back wall, angling his feet so his toes didn't poke out into the corridor.

There were some shouts from outside. Something went *pu-plllushk* and Denzel's hair stood on end like he'd been electrocuted. The church walls trembled. There was a sound like a disappointed firework.

And then there was nothing but the wheezing of Denzel's breathing, and the rhythmic thud-thud-thudding of his heart.

Several long moments crept by. Denzel peeked his head out of the alcove then immediately pulled it back in. He saw nothing, although he realised that was probably because he'd moved far too quickly, and had been blinking quite rapidly at the time.

Steeling himself, he tried again. This time, he leaned out from his hiding place much more slowly. Relief washed over him when he spotted the familiar Vulteron and Oberon uniforms approaching.

It drained away again just as quickly when he recognised the people wearing them.

"You can come out of there, Denzel," Knightley said. "We can see you."

She'd been looking directly at him, but Denzel pressed

himself back into the shadows anyway. He couldn't really think of anything else to do. At least, nothing that didn't involve soiling himself and fainting, which he wasn't ruling out at this stage.

Knightley and Rasmus stopped in front of him. Denzel smiled awkwardly. "Oh, hey," he said. "Sorry, were you talking to me?"

"Samara and Boyle are in custody," Knightley said. "Come with us. We're taking you to Director Quinn."

Knightley had her guns lowered, and Rasmus was doing nothing but sneering down his long nose in Denzel's direction. Neither of them considered him a threat, and that, Denzel decided, would be their undoing!

He clenched his fist.

He raised his arm.

"Flereous!" he cried, pointing the ring at them.

Nothing happened.

Denzel tutted and lowered his arm again. "Oh well. It was worth a try."

Knightley turned to Rasmus. "Would you consider that resisting arrest?"

Rasmus nodded slowly. "Oh yes. Definitely. Strongly resisting arrest."

Knightley thumbed a switch on the side of one of her pistols. It hummed ominously. She raised it until it was pointed right at the middle of Denzel's chest.

"Yeah, that's what I thought," Knightley said. Something mean glinted behind her eyes. "Brace yourself, Denzel. This is probably going to hurt."

Denzel tensed. He screwed his eyes tightly shut, bracing himself as he waited for the pain.

And waited.

And waited.

It was taking quite a long time, he realised.

Denzel opened one eye. It was so surprised by what it saw, it made the other one open, too, so it could double-check.

Knightley and Rasmus were on the floor, unconscious. A figure was sticking half-out of the wall behind them, its upper body visible, its lower half somewhere on the other side of the masonry. It was, quite unmistakably, a ghost.

It was also, quite unmistakably, something else.

Denzel's jaw dropped. "Smithy?" he whispered.

Halfway through the wall, Smithy smiled. "Hey, Denzel," he said. "Surprise!"

Smithy leaned over and caught Denzel by the wrist. "I should warn you, this might be a bit unpleasant," he announced, then he yanked Denzel hard, and pulled him straight through the wall.

CHAPTER 17

Passing through the wall wasn't that unpleasant for Denzel. Losing his balance and smashing his face against the floor in the storeroom next door, on the other hand, was. Once he'd recovered, Denzel rolled on to his back and kicked across the bare floorboards, putting as much distance between himself and Smithy as possible.

"Sorry," Smithy said. "Probably shouldn't have let you go so quickly."

Denzel shook from head to toe. His jaw flapped as he struggled to make sense of the jumble of thoughts racing around inside his head.

"Smithy. You're a... You're a..."

"A ghost," said Smithy. "Yeah."

"But, I mean... I mean... You're a *ghost*."

"Yep."

"You're a ghost, Smithy!"

"Think we've officially established that now," Smithy said.

"But... But... But..."

Smithy leaned down and slapped Denzel across the face. Denzel stopped shaking. He swallowed. "Thanks."

"No worries," said Smithy.

Denzel stood up, still keeping his distance. Now that he wasn't poking through a wall, Smithy didn't look any different to how he usually looked. There was no ghostly blue glow, he wasn't transparent, and his feet were firmly on the floor. He was just Smithy.

Smithy the ghost.

"So ... what?" Denzel said. "You're dead?"

"Mostly, yep," Smithy said.

A horrible thought occurred to Denzel. "Did they kill you? The Spectre Collectors?"

Smithy shook his head. "No. I was dead before we met them."

"Well... Since when, then?"

Smithy scratched his head. "What day is it today?"

"Saturday," said Denzel.

"Saturday the...?"

"Sixteenth," said Denzel.

"Of...?"

"June," said Denzel.

"Right." Smithy counted on his fingers and mumbled below his breath. "Since 1681," he announced.

"*You've been dead since 1681*?" Denzel spluttered. "Why didn't you tell me?"

Smithy frowned. "You hadn't been born."

"No, I mean now. Recently. At school. Why didn't you tell me then?"

"Dunno." Smithy shrugged. "Didn't think you'd be that interested."

Denzel gaped. "You didn't think I'd be that interested that *you're a ghost*?"

"Yeah," said Smithy. "I mean, it's not like it would change anything, is it?"

"Are you nuts?" Denzel yelped. "It'd change *everything*!"

Smithy looked down at his feet. "Yeah," he said, his voice uncharacteristically quiet. "Well, maybe that's why I didn't tell you."

"You lied to me, Smithy," Denzel said. "I thought you were, I don't know, normal! Well, I mean, not *normal*, exactly, but not ... not ... dead!"

Smithy said nothing, just kept staring down at his feet.

"I'm sorry," he eventually whispered.

"You're a ghost, Smithy!"

"Yep," Smithy said. "I'm a ghost."

"You're a four-dimensional Corporeal! Or whatever they're called."

"Am I?" said Smithy. He puffed out his cheeks. "That's a new one on me."

Denzel looked him up and down. A ghost. His best friend — arguably his only friend — was a ghost. He'd hidden it from him, lied to him for all these months.

"I guess this means you probably don't want to hang out any more," said Smithy. "It's OK. I understand. I'm a ghost and you're the ghost police, or whatever."

Denzel shook his head, still barely able to believe it. "Look. I'm going to ask you one question, Smithy, and I want you to give me an honest answer," he said.

Smithy nodded, still not looking up. "OK," he whispered, his voice cracking.

"The truth, remember?" Denzel said. "No more lies. No more pretending."

Smithy nodded again.

"OK, here goes," Denzel began. He cleared his throat. He took a deep breath. "What would you rather have, right?"

Smithy raised his eyes.

"A tongue made of never-ending toffee..."

A smile tugged at the corner of Smithy's mouth.

"...or Godzilla for a pet?"

"Easy," said Smithy, snorting through his mucus plugs. "Tongue made of toffee."

"What?! Are you nuts?" Denzel asked. "No way. Godzilla for a pet!"

"But where would you keep him?" Smithy said. "Your garden's tiny."

"I'd build him a kennel," Denzel said. "And a really massive cat flap in the kitchen door."

Smithy rolled his eyes. "Well, while you're doing that, I'll be enjoying the smooth, sweet taste of toffee twenty-four hours a day, seven days a week."

Denzel laughed. Properly laughed. It was the first time since before the trash-monster. It felt good.

"You're a ghost, Smithy," he said, once he'd stopped laughing. "An actual *ghost*!"

"Yep," Smithy said. He smiled. "Still me, though."

"But ... how?"

Smithy shrugged. "Same as most of them, really. I died, but couldn't find my way into the Spectral Realm. I kept looking for a couple of hundred years, then gave up."

"And so you decided to go to school?"

"I don't go to school," Smithy said. "I just spotted you on the wall one day and thought I'd say hello. You seemed all right, so I kept coming back."

Denzel thought back. He'd never actually seen Smithy inside the school, much less in any classes.

"Wait, if you're a ghost, then how come you're always eating my lunch?"

"You keep offering," Smithy said. "Felt a bit rude to say no. Anyway, some of your sandwiches were quite nice, once I picked off the green stuff."

"No, but ... you're a ghost. Ghosts don't eat!"

"Some of us do," Smithy said. "I mean, we don't have to, but some of us quite enjoy it."

"But why doesn't it just pass through you?"

Smithy grinned. "It does. Eventually." He shrugged. "I haven't met many other ghosts, so I don't know how everything works. Me, I can be completely solid, and pretty much pass myself off as still being alive. On the other hand, I can walk through walls, but only if I decide to. That took practice."

"How much practice?" Denzel asked.

"About three hundred years."

"Wow."

"Give or take a decade."

"Right," said Denzel. "So... Aren't you all, like ... *evil*? That's what the Spectre Collectors think."

"Don't think so," said Smithy. "Although I do sometimes sneak into the cinema without paying. Does that count?"

There was a commotion from beyond the storeroom door. Smithy grabbed Denzel by the wrist again. "Come on, we'd better go," he urged. Denzel held his breath as Smithy pulled him through the back wall, and this time managed to stay on his feet when he stumbled out through the other side.

"That is pretty handy," Denzel admitted. They had emerged into a small graveyard at the side of the church. Denzel could hear voices around the corner at the front, and got the impression there were lots of people gathering there, none of whom sounded particularly friendly.

"Come on, we can get through the graveyard wall and on to the street that way," said Smithy.

"Then what?" asked Denzel.

"I thought we could move to Las Vegas and become professional gamblers," Smithy said. "They'll call me Snake-Hands Smithy, and you'll be Jimmy the Shoes."

"Why would they call me Jimmy the Shoes?" asked Denzel.

"Why wouldn't they?"

"Because my name's not Jimmy," Denzel pointed out.

"You do wear shoes, though," said Smithy.

Denzel frowned. "Yeah, but..." He shook his head. Now wasn't the time to argue with Smithy Logic. "We can't do that, anyway. We can't run away."

"We definitely can," said Smithy. "It's easy, look." He mimed running in slow motion. "It's like that, only faster."

"No, I mean we have to go back," Denzel said. "Quinn has Samara and Boyle."

"Is that the same Samara and Boyle who kidnapped us and threw us in their van?" Smithy asked.

"Yes!"

"And threatened to shoot us. Several times," Smithy said. "The Samara and Boyle who have dedicated their lives to hunting ghosts. That's the Samara and Boyle you want to go back and rescue?"

Denzel nodded. "They're not the bad guys," he insisted. "They helped me. They're trying to stop Quinn."

"Stop her doing what?"

"She's got a machine," Denzel said. "She's planning to punch a hole into the Spectral Realm and suck up all the ghosts, but it's going to destroy the world. At least, that's what the poltergeist told me."

He shuddered. "And when I say it 'told me' I mean it put its tentacles inside my head and fed the images directly into my brain."

"That's poltergeists for you," said Smithy. "Probably. I've never actually seen one. As far as I know, not even other poltergeists can see them."

Denzel frowned. "So how come I can?"

Smithy shrugged. "Beats me." He blew out his cheeks and looked back at the church. "You really want to go back down there?"

"I have to try to stop her," Denzel said. "But you don't. It'll be too dangerous. They'll detect you."

"Haven't detected me so far," said Smithy. He puffed up his chest. "Anyway, I'm all about danger," he said. "I eat danger for breakfast. Danger's my middle name."

"OK…"

"Absolutely none of that's true, by the way," Smith said. "I just said it all to try to make myself seem much more impressive." He grinned broadly. "Still, I'm dead. What's the worst that can happen?"

CHAPTER 18

Denzel held his breath as he was *whooshed* through another wall. This time, he emerged at the top of a curved stone staircase that twisted down into a gloomy half-darkness far below.

"These stairs take you down to their headquarters," Smithy announced. His voice echoed loudly and he quickly clamped a hand over his mouth.

"How do you know?" Denzel whispered.

"I've been hanging about since I left," Smithy said. "Thought I'd snoop around a bit in case you got into trouble." He pointed down the steps. "I'll go ahead and check the coast's clear."

"What if they see you?" Denzel asked.

Smithy winked. "How will they see me when I do this?" he asked, then he pursed his lips, clenched his fists and furrowed his brow in concentration.

"Do what?" Denzel asked.

"I'm turning invisible," Smithy said, starting to shake from the effort.

"You're turning purple," Denzel corrected.

"Never have got the hang of that," Smithy sighed. "If anyone's coming, I'll duck through the wall." He began to tiptoe ahead. "I'll shout if it's clear."

"Don't shout," Denzel said. "That'll attract attention. Do, I don't know, a bird sound or something."

Smithy nodded. "Bird sound. Gotcha."

He set off down the steps. Denzel hung back, listening. There was a door right beside him that he guessed led back into the church. He jammed a foot against the bottom of it, in case someone tried to open it from the other side.

"Har-ooook! *Har-ooook!*"

Denzel jumped with fright at the high-pitched cry from below. He scurried down the spiral steps and caught up with Smithy after several turns. "What was that?" he whispered. "I said make a bird noise."

"That was a bird noise," said Smithy. "It was a heron."

"Well, don't do a heron!" Denzel told him. "Do a normal bird!"

Smithy nodded. "Right. Will do."

He scampered down the stairs again. Denzel waited. There was silence for a moment, broken eventually by a solitary "Quack".

Denzel rolled his eyes. "It's an improvement, I suppose."

They continued down for several minutes, with Smithy quacking, tweeting and occasionally honking all the way to the bottom.

The door at the bottom of the steps looked old, with black metal bands running across it. There was no handle, just a retina scanner fixed at eye-height on to the wood.

"Where does it lead?" Denzel whispered.

"Dunno," Smithy said. "I never came all the way down this way. Want me to nip through and check?"

"We'll go together," Denzel said. "It's more dangerous for you in there than it is for me."

"Oh, I don't know," said Smithy. "They could do all sorts to you."

"Well, yeah," Denzel admitted.

"Chop your hands off. Smash your toes with a hammer..."

"Why would they do that?" Denzel said. "They

wouldn't do that!"

"Pop out your eyes…"

"They're not going to do any of that," Denzel hissed. At least, he hoped not. He held a hand out. "Now, come on, let's sneak through, find Samara and Boyle, then we'll take Quinn by surprise."

Smithy nodded. "Foolproof plan," he said, taking Denzel by the wrist. They floated through the door and into an all-too-familiar office on the other side.

"Come in, Denzel," said Quinn. "We've been waiting for you."

Smithy looked sideways at Denzel. "OK, maybe not *one hundred per cent* foolproof, but it was still a solid plan." He shrugged. "You know. Ish."

Quinn sat facing the door in her high-backed leather chair, legs neatly crossed, a cup of tea balanced on a saucer in her hand. Knightley and Rasmus stood either side of her, guns and hands pointed at the new arrivals.

"Cor, them two move quick, don't they?" said Smithy.

Quinn's eyes went to Smithy, then opened a fraction in surprise. "What is he doing here? How can he be here? He can't remember you."

"He does," said Denzel.

"I do," confirmed Smithy. "You know what they say. Elephants never—"

"Not now, Smithy," said Denzel.

Quinn looked Smithy up and down. "Oh my. You're a Corporeal Four-Dimensional Non-Mortal Entity."

"If you say so, love," said Smithy.

"Of course," she whispered. "How could I not have seen it?"

"What have you done with Samara and Boyle?" Denzel demanded.

"They went AWOL. I had them arrested," Quinn said, tearing her eyes away from Smithy. She stood up, waved a hand above the cup and saucer, and made them disappear. "You're wrong, you know, Denzel. About my machine," she said. "It's not dangerous. It's a force for good. It's going to make the world a better place."

"It isn't," Denzel insisted. "I've seen what happens. The poltergeist showed me."

Quinn let out the least amused-sounding "Ha!" in the history of the world. "Oh, so a malevolent supernatural entity showed you, did it?" she asked. "An unfeeling creature that would, given half a chance, destroy each and every one of us, warned you it was dangerous?"

She looked Denzel up and down. "And here I thought you were supposed to see things more clearly than the rest of us. How disappointing."

Quinn turned. Her chair rolled out of her path

seemingly of its own accord. "Bring them," she commanded, striding towards the door leading out into the main complex. "It's time for the demonstration."

Denzel and Smithy stood in the centre of a vast, warehouse-like room, flanked on both sides by Spectre Collectors. On the right, a regiment of around eighty Vulterons stood snapped to attention. Looking far more relaxed on Denzel's left were about the same number of Oberons, all wearing matching robes.

Samara and Boyle knelt on the floor between Denzel and Quinn, their hands cuffed behind their backs, gags pulled tightly across the mouths. From behind, Denzel could see that all of Samara's rings were missing. Instinctively, he felt for the Feurety Ring on his own finger, and wondered if he could somehow pass it to her without anyone noticing.

All eyes were on Quinn, who stood like a queen holding court. Knightley and Rasmus were beside her, keeping a close watch over the prisoners.

Behind them all, towering above the crowd, stood the Spook Suit. There was a scratch on its paintwork that matched pretty much perfectly with a scrape on the ceiling high overhead. Denzel pretended not to notice, and hoped no one else did, either.

SPECTRE COLLECTORS

"Cor, what does that thing do?" Smithy whispered.

"What *doesn't* it do?" replied Denzel.

"The ironing?" Smithy guessed.

"No, I doubt it does that," Denzel admitted.

"Soldiers of the Seventh Army of the Enlightened," Quinn began. Her voice seemed to expand to fill the vast room. She gazed across the faces of the teenagers watching her and smiled her textbook smile. "Friends."

There was an appreciative murmur from the Oberons. Quinn waited for it to die down, before continuing. "For centuries, the Cult of Sh'grath has worked tirelessly to protect the planet from spooks, spectres and things that go bump in the night.

"We have dedicated ourselves to ridding this world of entities which would seek to do it harm." Her expression and her voice both turned cold. "And for what purpose?" she asked. She cast her eyes across the audience, but no one volunteered an answer.

"Each year, we capture hundreds of them. Thousands. And each year thousands more creep out of the shadows like vermin, and the battle starts all over again. How many partners have we lost? Friends? Loved ones? And how many more must be lose before we start to take matters more seriously?"

"What do you mean?" asked an Oberon.

"I mean the end of our ongoing war," Quinn announced. "And the birth of a brave new world! A world where we no longer have to sacrifice our lives and the lives of our children to help defend a world that doesn't know or care about us. Behold!"

She raised her arms and a section of floor slid away in front of her. A rack of willow-bound gemstones rose up out of the ground, along with a desktop-computer-sized machine that managed to look both horribly cumbersome and perfectly sleek at the same time.

"I bet that's it," Denzel whispered. "That's the Spectral Disruptor."

A low-level muttering broke out on both sides of the room as the rack and the device came to a stop. Quinn rocked back on her heels, allowing the chatter to build.

Smithy leaned closer to Denzel. "I will say this for her, she's an excellent public speaker," he whispered. "Really confident."

"Completely mental, though," said Denzel.

"Oh yeah. Definitely," Smithy agreed. "Mad as a box of frogs."

"For generations we have strived. Endlessly. Thanklessly. Protecting the world from threats it wasn't even aware existed," Quinn boomed. "We have put away thousands, but how many other entities are out there?

Millions? Billions? They are a disease. A cancer. And we have been nothing but a sticking plaster."

"Amen, sister!" hollered Smithy. All eyes turned to him. He blushed. "Sorry. Carry on." He glanced at Denzel. "Got caught up in it there. She's really quite persuasive."

"I know," Denzel agreed. "After I came back she put me under some kind of hypnotism or..."

His eyes went to Knightley and Rasmus, then to the other Spectre Collectors standing on either side. How many of those were under Quinn's thrall? Not all of them, or there would be no need for the speech, but some of them, probably.

"That changes today," Quinn said. She plucked a gemstone from the rack and fed it into something that looked like a loading tube on the side of the machine. "Today, we send them all away. We pack every last spook, spectre and spirit off to where it belongs. The Spectral Realm!"

Another wave of murmuring rippled around the room. Quinn ran her fingertips over the machine's surface. A series of runes glowed faintly across the metal and a high-pitched whine resonated around the room.

"Bet she says 'behold' again," Smithy whispered.

"Behold!" Quinn cried.

"Told you."

The surface of the machine began to crackle and spark. Quinn's face was a mask of excited glee, her eyes almost bulging in anticipation of what was to come.

On both sides, the assembled Spectre Collectors shuffled backwards. Even Knightley and Rasmus looked uncertain as the device began to vibrate across the floor.

"Everybody stay where you are!" Quinn ordered. "You are witnessing the beginning of a brave new world!"

"The beginning of the end, more like," Denzel whispered. He leaned closer to Smithy. "Can you free Samara and Boyle?"

"Definitely," Smithy said. "Or probably." He shrugged. "I can give it a go."

"You can do it," Denzel said. "I need to stop her loading any more gems into that machine."

"How?"

"I'm going to think of a word," said Denzel.

Smithy frowned. "What word?"

Denzel closed his eyes.

He thought of a word.

"Flereous," he whispered.

There was a spark. A whoosh.

And a jet of flame erupted across the room.

CHAPTER 19

Quinn waved a hand and the flames died away. Denzel hissed in pain as the ring on his finger turned icy cold, then shattered and fell off.

The director's half-smile crept across her face again. "Almost impressive. But you missed me, Denzel," she said.

Denzel shook his head. "No, I didn't."

Quinn frowned. "Sorry to break it to you, but clearly you did."

"Nope. For me to have missed you, I'd have had to be aiming at you in the first place," Denzel said. "But I wasn't."

Quinn continued to look confused for a moment, then one of her nostrils turned upwards. She sniffed.

"You probably recognise that smell," Denzel said. "I bet you're trying to remember what it is. I'll tell you. It's burning willow."

Quinn's head snapped to her left. The willow branches around each of the gems were blackened and charred. "No!" she yelped, making a grab for the closest gem just as the others began to tremble and shake.

With a furious roar, Quinn slammed the gem into the loading tube of her machine. The whine reached an ear-splitting pitch, and the air around it seemed to bubble and bulge.

The assembled Spectre Collectors watched on in amazement as a thin line of purple light stretched upwards from the machine. The world itself seemed to part, just a fraction, as if a zip were being undone.

"Now, Smithy!" Denzel yelped, but Smithy was staring into the widening gap, transfixed by the swirling kaleidoscope of colours beyond.

"Is that... Is that the Spectral Realm?" he asked no one in particular. "It's beautiful."

"Smithy!" said Denzel. "Samara and Boyle. Quick!"

Smithy gave himself a shake and dropped to his knees. "Hi, I'm Smithy, we met before when you kidnapped me, remember?" he said, looking at Boyle in particular. "You were actually quite mean to me. But that's in the past. Bygones. Oh, and guess what? I'm a ghost. Surprise!"

He pressed a hand on both their heads. There was a *clink* as their handcuffs and gags passed cleanly through their bodies and landed on the ground. "Cool, huh?" Smithy grinned.

Boyle and Samara jumped to their feet just as bolts of purple lightning spat from inside the Spectral Realm and licked across the ceiling. There was a commotion on either side of the room as the assembled Spectre Collectors all tried to put distance between themselves and the hole.

"I'm guessing it's not supposed to be doing that," Denzel said.

Samara shook her head. "It's unstable. If we don't shut it down, I think it'll keep growing."

"Knightley!" Boyle barked. "Give me a gun."

Knightley looked at him in surprise, then back at the shuddering machine.

"Whatever she told you she was doing, whatever she said, it isn't going to work, Knightley!" Boyle roared. "So give me a gun. Now!"

With a shaky nod, Knightley tossed one of her handguns to Boyle. He snatched it from the air and unleashed a volley of laser fire on Quinn's device. The top of the machine exploded, sending plumes of red smoke into the air. There was an audible *rrrrrip* as the hole into the Spectral Realm grew wider.

Smithy sidled up to Boyle. "Hate to say it, but that just made it worse, if anything."

"Uh, guys," said Denzel, his voice shaking. Two clawed hands, each finger as long as a fully grown man, appeared through the gap. They pressed against the edges of the hole, slowly but surely forcing it wider. "What's that?"

"Nothing good," Samara gulped. She spun to face the hastily retreating Oberons. "Rasmus. Everyone. We need to close this up!"

Boyle turned to the other side of the room. "And we need to keep that thing back until they do. Move, move, move!"

For a moment, nobody moved. Then, a few of the Spectre Collectors on either side found their nerve and hurried towards the middle of the room. Others followed, and soon a large crowd was forming around the tear.

Denzel and Smithy found themselves nudged out of the way. Smithy was still mesmerised by the swirling colours inside the hole. He had a goofy grin plastered across his face most of the time, but right now it was the goofiest Denzel had ever seen it.

"The Spectral Realm," Smithy whispered. "After all these years, I've actually found the Spectral Realm."

"I should help them," Denzel said. "I should do something."

Smithy blinked. "What? What can you do?"

"The Spook Suit!" Denzel cried. "I can use that!"

He turned in the direction of the battle armour, then an enormous metal hand swatted him, sending him tumbling across the room.

Denzel smashed into the rack of gems, scattering them across the floor. He sank to the ground, groaning and clutching his ribs.

"Sorry, were you looking for *this*?"

There was a *whirr* and a *clank* as the Spook Suit closed in on him. Denzel looked to Samara and Boyle, but they were focused on stopping the giant … whatever-it-was escaping the Spectral Realm, and hadn't even noticed his predicament.

"You ruined it," hissed Quinn's voice from inside the robot battle suit. "You ruined everything!"

"Me? What did I do?" Denzel yelped.

"You sabotaged my machine," Quinn growled.

"No, I didn't! I wouldn't know where to start!" Denzel protested. He pointed over to the rip in reality.

The clawed hands were still working to push it apart. "Shouldn't you be stopping that thing?"

"Oh, what's the point?" Quinn snapped. "It's not like anyone will thank me for it. No one ever does. Let it come, I say. Let them all come. One way or another, this pointless, never-ending war ends today."

Smithy stepped in front of the fallen Denzel and pointed up towards the Spook Suit's glass head. "Hey, back off, lady. Leave my friend—"

An enormous foot slammed down on Smithy, squashing him. "Smithy!" Denzel cried.

"I'm OK. I'm fine, I'm fine," came a muffled voice from below the foot. "Flatter than I'd like, but I'm OK."

The Spook Suit raised a fist. "Let's see if you're as resilient as your friend is, Denzel," Quinn spat. The fist arced down. Denzel threw up his arms in a desperate attempt to protect himself.

Beside him, something black and smoke-like billowed out from inside a gem.

The poltergeist wrapped around him just as the fist connected. The impact of the blow was powerful, yet surprisingly gentle at the same time, like being hit by a pillow travelling at a hundred and seventy miles per hour.

Quinn drew back the robotic fist and stared down at

Denzel. Unable to see the poltergeist, she had no idea why he wasn't now just a ketchup-like splodge on the floor.

"What...? How did you...?" she said.

The 'geist wrapped its tendrils around Denzel's arms and legs, then hoisted him into a standing position. The other gems rattled and rolled across the floor. Denzel watched in amazement as wispy shapes snaked out of the stones. They circled around him, then seemed to fold themselves into the poltergeist until Denzel was completely surrounded by a suit of ghosts.

No, not a suit, he realised.

An armour.

"Room for a small one?" asked Smithy, rising up through the floor next to Denzel. His face was an enormous circle, his stamped-on head now only a few centimetres thick. He turned wispy at the edges, gave Denzel a wink, then merged with the ghost armour.

Denzel couldn't see the smoky black of the poltergeist now. Instead, he was surrounded by something he couldn't quite describe. It was as if a crystal had become a liquid and a gas at the same time, while somehow managing to stay completely solid. It glinted in the glow of the purple lightning and the flickering blasts of the Spectre Collectors' magic and gunfire.

Denzel grinned. He flexed his muscles, and the ghosts flexed with him. He'd never felt anything like it. He felt powerful! Indestructible! Unstoppable!

A metal foot toe-punted him and he hurtled, screaming, across the room. He smashed against the heavy doors of the Advanced Weapons Vault, buckling them. "Ow," he groaned, as he slid to the ground.

His legs moved on their own, flipping him back on to his feet like a kung fu master showing off at a party. He flew – not ran or jumped, but actually flew – towards the Spook Suit. He felt his arm draw back, saw the ghosts bunch into an enormous fist around his hand.

The sound of the uppercut echoed around the warehouse, loud enough to drown out everything else. The force of the punch lifted the Spook Suit off its feet. It landed heavily on several racks of shelving, crushing them beneath its immense weight.

Denzel giggled. He couldn't help himself. "OK, so that was pretty cool!"

"You know what else is pretty cool?" said Smithy's voice from somewhere inside the ghost armour. "My butt's in your face."

"Ew, Smithy!" Denzel spluttered.

"Just kidding," said Smithy. "I don't currently have a butt."

Denzel breathed a sigh of relief.

"But if I did, it'd totally be in your face right now."

The Spook Suit lay motionless on the floor. Denzel started to move closer, and the suit of ghosts followed. "Did we do it?" he asked. "Did we knock her out?"

"Down, maybe," crackled Quinn's voice from within the suit. Two of its four feet clamped around Denzel. The robotic head raised. "But not out."

The legs snapped upwards, launching Denzel towards the ceiling. He flailed wildly as he hurtled through the air, then hit the roof with a *thud*. Before he could start to fall, Quinn was rocketing towards him in the suit, fist drawn back.

BOOM! A punch drove him through the ceiling and the floor of the corridor above. He turned to run, but a robotic hand clamped around his leg and tore him back down through the floor again.

Denzel and Smithy both let out a long, panicked howl as Quinn swung Denzel around, then hurled him back up towards the ceiling. He spun, flipping and twirling out of control, his arms flapping frantically like a bird.

"Ooh, this is so going to hurt," he grimaced, but instead of smashing into the roof, he passed cleanly through it like a ghost.

The momentum of the throw carried him through

several other rooms and corridors, before he emerged through the surface of the church car park and came to a stop several metres into the air.

Although Denzel had stopped, the world continued to spin unpleasantly. "Ugh. I think I'm going to throw up," he groaned.

"Don't you dare!" warned Smithy. "Seriously, I think I speak for all of us in here when I say we wouldn't be happy."

Before Denzel could reply, the ground began to shake. The church, already damaged from the earlier battle, folded like a house of cards as a monstrous metal shape erupted through the car park.

Quinn snarled up through the Spook Suit's glass visor. "Face me, Denzel," she said. "Face me and *die!*"

CHAPTER 20

Smoke and fire belched out of the Spook Suit's boots as it propelled itself into the sky. Denzel tried to run away, but this was made difficult by his being in mid-air. He jogged on the spot for a few awkward moments before the ghosts figured out what he was trying to do.

The world lurched and he shot off across the sky, leaving his stomach somewhere far behind.

"I'm flying!" he yelped, gazing down at the town spread out below him. He recognised a few landmarks as he hurtled above them. There was the shopping centre, the park, his school. Instinctively, he turned to look for his house, then he cried out in shock as a fist slammed into him from above, sending him spiralling towards the ground.

He hit the ground like a meteorite, smashing a spider's web pattern into the surface of the road, and toppling a delivery van that stood idling nearby. All along the street, people began to scream and run for cover.

Denzel stood up, wincing with the pain it brought. He'd felt that one, even through the ghost-armour.

The ground beside him erupted in a rain of fire. He stumbled back, so dazzled by the glare of the blasts that he didn't see the fist swinging towards him until it was too late.

With an ear-splitting *smash*, Denzel rocketed through the wall of a terraced house and came to rest in a small, cluttered sitting room. An old woman with thin grey hair and thick gold glasses peered at him over her knitting.

"Sorry," Denzel mumbled, then his legs kicked and he launched himself back out on to the street.

WHAM! He drove both fists into the Spook Suit's head. It staggered backwards, arms flailing as it fought to stay upright. Denzel drew back with another ghost-powered punch, but a robotic foot swung up and slammed into his chest before he could connect.

Quinn brought an arm up over the suit's head and swatted Denzel back down on to the ground. The hand clamped down on top of him, pinning him to the road.

"Why are you doing this?" Denzel asked. "It doesn't make sense!"

"You know what doesn't make sense, Denzel?" Quinn spat. "Taking a four-year-old girl and hiding her away from the world! Shipping her from underground bunker to underground bunker while you train her for a war she never wanted any part of!"

"Wow, she's got some serious issues," Smithy whispered. "Oh, and P.S., I can see right up her nose from here."

"I've lost count of the number of times I've saved the world over the years, and for what? What was the point? Did anyone ever thank me? Did anyone even know what I'd done?" Quinn demanded. "Of course not, because it had to be kept a *secret*."

The other robotic arm extended, gesturing to the crowd of onlookers cowering at the far end of the street. "Well, the secret's finally out!"

The cannons on the Spook Suit's shoulders swivelled down and took aim. "I just wanted a normal life, that's all. But it looks like that's not going to happen," she said. She leaned down until her face behind the visor was the only thing Denzel could see. "So if I can't have it, no one can."

Both cannons opened fire. Denzel gasped as the ghost-armour sunk backwards through the ground to safety.

"Thanks," he managed, before the surface of the road exploded, and the Spook Suit loomed above him again.

"You can't escape me, Denzel," Quinn hissed. "This thing can track your every move. It's the ultimate weapon, completely unstoppable."

"No, it's not," Denzel realised. "There's something even more powerful."

"The power of friendship!" Smithy cried.

Denzel ignored him. "The time bomb."

"That was going to be my next guess," said Smithy.

Quinn's face fell. "You wouldn't dare."

"Let's find out," said Denzel, then he spun on to his feet, bounded twice along the street, and launched himself over the heads of the screaming crowd below.

Denzel rocketed across the sky, sending a sonic boom rolling off in all directions. In seconds, he could see the church again, or what was left of it, at least. His heart soared. He was going to make it. He was going to make it!

"Crazy lady at six o'clock!" Smithy cried.

The ghost-armour banked Denzel sharply to the right, dodging a rocket that whistled past. A jet of blue flame erupted from the Spook Suit's left shoulder-cannon – the one Boyle had boasted could shoot gods. The air around Denzel crackled and scorched, and the ghosts all wailed and writhed in pain.

The punches, explosions and high-speed pavement collisions hadn't hurt the ghosts, but whatever the blue flame was, the effect was instantaneous. The shimmering glow of the armour flickered, and Denzel suddenly found himself at the mercy of gravity again. He plummeted down, down, down, screaming as he fell.

"Smithy! Smithy, what's happening?"

Somewhere inside the armour, Smithy groaned. An indistinct ghostly shape peeled away from Denzel. Then another. Then another. As more and more spirits left Denzel's protective coating, the faster he fell.

"Smithy? Smithy, are you still with me?" Denzel shouted.

The only reply from Smithy was another sleepy moan. The road was racing up to meet them, and impact was only a few seconds away.

"Smithy, what would you rather do, right?" Denzel cried. "Wake up right now, or let your best friend splatter against the—"

Denzel suddenly changed direction. He heard Smithy grit his teeth, which, considering Smithy didn't currently have any teeth, was really quite impressive. They were still falling, but now they were falling backwards towards the hole in the church car park.

Quinn roared towards them in the Spook Suit, the rocket boots churning the air behind it. More blue flame billowed from one of the guns on her shoulder. It flared around Denzel like a cocoon, the heat searing his skin and scorching his eyebrows.

Suddenly, Denzel could see the black tendrils of the poltergeist again. He watched them unravel from him one by one, before the 'geist was whipped away by the wind.

With a start, Denzel realised the armour had gone. He was free-falling, the air ruffling his hair and flapping his clothes as he plunged helplessly through the hole the Spook Suit had torn through the Spectre Collectors' HQ.

A pair of arms wrapped feebly around him from behind. "Hold on," Smithy whispered.

"To what?" Denzel yelped.

"Good point," said Smithy. "Well made."

His arms went limp.

Denzel tensed.

There was a *boom* as they hit the floor.

CHAPTER 21

Denzel's eyelids fluttered.

There was quite a lot of noise going on. Shouts. Explosions. The high-pitched whine of laser fire.

That sort of thing.

Part of his brain was telling him he should open his eyes and get up, but another, much larger, part reckoned that probably wouldn't be in his best interests.

He opened them anyway.

The rip leading through to the Spectral Realm was still there, he noted, almost absent-mindedly. The enormous clawed hands had gone, though, so that was nice. The entire squadron of Vulterons was pumping round after round of gunfire into the hole, while dozens of Oberons wove their hands through the air as they worked to knit the tear back together.

It wasn't something you got to see every day, and Denzel would've quite liked to just lie there and watch it all unfolding, but he had a nagging thought that he was supposed to be doing something else. Something important.

An enormous robot battle suit dropped from the sky and landed on its four feet beside him.

Oh, yes. That was it.

"Waaaargh!" Denzel kicked frantically, scrambling backwards across the floor. He looked around for Smithy, but his friend was nowhere to be seen.

Quinn advanced and the floor trembled with every footstep. "It's almost going to be a shame to kill you, Denzel," she crackled through the suit's speakers. "You really are fascinating. You would have been a valuable ally, going forward, and we never did find out how you could see poltergeists. How *can* you do that, by the way?"

Denzel's back hit the metal door of the vault. He stopped. There's was nowhere left to go. "I don't know," Denzel admitted. "But even if I did, I wouldn't tell you."

The Spook Suit shrugged along with its occupant.

"Honestly? I don't care any more. You've ruined everything. And now you're going to pay."

Something flat and smooth, like a large silver pebble, emerged through the door of the vault, followed a moment later by a familiar face. "Is this the bomb thing you were after?" Smithy asked.

Quinn stumbled backwards. "Don't! Don't touch that!"

"I reckon that's probably a 'yes', then," said Denzel. He stood and took the time bomb from Smithy. It was a small circle, and easily fit in his two hands, but the weight of it pushed his arms down.

"Cor," he said, pretending to drop it. "It's heavier than it looks, innit?"

"Stop it!" Quinn hissed. "You have no idea what it could do!"

"Yeah, but neither do you, do you?" Denzel said. He smiled calmly up at her. "Why don't we find out together?"

"No!" Quinn said. "It could destroy us all! It could shatter time itself!"

"It might, yeah," Denzel said. He waved the time bomb in her direction. "So you'd better surrender now, Quinn."

Quinn nodded slowly. "I suppose I better had," she said. She held her robotic arms out in front of her, as if waiting for handcuffs to be slapped on. "I mean, obviously you must know all the necessary incantations required to activate it."

Denzel shuffled awkwardly. He swallowed. "Hmm?" he said.

"The incantations required to activate the Quantum Nullifier," Quinn said. A smirk tugged at the corners of her mouth. "I'm assuming you've learned them all."

Denzel nodded, his throat suddenly dry. "Yep," he said. "Definitely know all them."

Quinn's laugh spat at him through the suit's speakers. "Idiot child," she sneered. "Did you really think you could threaten me with something you don't even understand?"

"Probably not," Denzel admitted. "But then I wasn't threatening you with it. Not really. I was distracting you with it."

Quinn snorted. "Distracting me? From what?"

"From him," said Denzel, pointing to Quinn's left. The director turned and let out a gasp of shock.

"Cosy in here, innit?" Smithy said, tucked into the suit right beside her. He grinned, then held up a handful of something that looked a lot like glitter. The air above it seemed to shiver in anticipation.

Quinn's eyes went wide. She shook her head.

SPECTRE COLLECTORS

And Smithy blew.

"Almost out of ammo here!" Boyle warned, unleashing a volley of crackling energy into the narrowing void.

"Nearly … got it," Samara managed through gritted teeth. Two arcane symbols glowed blue in the palms of her hands. They left a sparkly trail as she waved them around, and she began chanting under her breath.

Behind her, dozens of other Oberons were doing the same, all moving in perfect time, their voices echoing as one.

Slowly – ever so slowly – the tear in reality began to close. Boyle and the other Vulterons kept firing for a few more seconds, before their weapons started to splutter and die.

Knightley reached to her belt for more ammunition, then groaned. "I'm out."

"Me too," Boyle announced, tossing her gun back.

"It's OK. We've got it," Samara said. "Closing in three … two…"

"Wait!"

Denzel stumbled over, pulling Smithy behind him. "Don't close it. Not yet," Denzel panted.

"What? Why?" Boyle demanded.

Denzel ignored him and turned to his friend. "The

Spectral Realm, Smithy," he said. "It's what you've been searching for, isn't it?"

Smithy stared in wonder at the swirling lightshow on the other side of the hole, like it was the most beautiful thing he had ever seen in his life. Or death, for that matter. The tear itself was barely a metre high now, but had stopped narrowing for the moment.

"Hurry up! We can't hold it like this for long," Rasmus warned.

"We'll hold it as long as we have to," Samara said.

Denzel put a hand on his friend's shoulder. "You've been alone for hundreds of years, looking to find your way here." He tried to smile, but his face was having none of it. His voice cracked. "You don't have to be alone any more, Smithy. You're home."

Smithy tore his eyes away from the Spectral Realm. He opened his mouth to speak, but the words wouldn't come. Instead, he threw his arms around Denzel and hugged him.

And then, pulling away from his friend, Smithy turned, at last, towards the light.

CHAPTER 22

Denzel stood between Samara and Boyle in Quinn's office, watching her work at her desk. She was drawing a fire engine in crayons.

"The thing with memory dust is that you have to really carefully measure it out," said Samara.

"Gotcha," said Denzel.

"Just a pinch is usually enough, unless you're trying to wipe decades off someone."

Denzel nodded. "Right."

"A big handful ... that's too much," Samara explained.

"Yep."

"Like, *waaaay* too much."

"Yep, I realise that now," said Denzel, watching Quinn stick her tongue out in concentration as she tried to colour within the lines. "What'll happen to her?"

"That's up to the Elders to decide," said Boyle. The office door swung open. Boyle snapped to attention. Even Samara straightened up. "Speaking of which, here they come now."

Three short figures entered, all dressed in matching purple robes that stretched from their necks to the floor, without any apparent holes for their arms to go through. Denzel frowned, then looked at both Samara and Boyle in turn. "Wait... That's the Elders?" he whispered.

"Yes," hissed Boyle through the side of his mouth.

Denzel looked the diminutive figures up and down. "Are you winding me up?" he said. "They look about nine."

"Ha! If only," laughed the lead Elder. She was the shortest of the bunch, and the only female of the group. Her eyes sparkled like blue gemstones, and her skin was smooth and flawless. "Very flattering of you, Denzel," she said. "But I assure you, we're much older than that."

"Twelve?" Denzel guessed, and the Elder woman smiled again.

"In centuries, perhaps."

She tilted her head from left to right, studying Denzel

closely. "I am sorry," she said.

"For what?" Denzel asked.

"For what was done to you. For what was taken from you, and from those who knew you."

Denzel nodded. "Uh, thanks," he said.

"You have a question you wish to ask me," the Elder said.

"No," said Denzel, frowning. "No, I don't really."

The Elder smiled. "Ask. Please."

Denzel swallowed. "Can you make them remember me?"

The Elder woman's smile didn't change shape, but somehow became sadder. "We cannot. I am so very sorry."

Denzel felt his eyes sting. He dug his fingernails into his palms. "Right," he managed. "Gotcha."

"But know, Denzel, that you will always have a home here," she said. Her smile widened, then fell away as she cast her gaze across at Quinn. "It seems we are in need of a new director for this chapter of the organisation."

Denzel blinked. His jaw dropped. "What … me?"

All three Elders snorted. "Ha! Oh my goodness, no," the leader said. "I'm sure we can find someone a little more experienced for the role."

"Oh, that's a relief," Denzel breathed. "I wouldn't

know where to start."

One of the male Elders leaned in and whispered in her head. She nodded slowly. "Yes, good point," she said, then she turned back to Denzel. "While we can't offer you the role of director – yet – there is the matter of placing you in a division."

She looked Samara and Boyle in turn. "Oberon or Vulteron? Has he shown any aptitude for either role?"

"None whatsoever, ma'am," said Boyle.

"Thanks a bunch," Denzel said.

"Not really," Samara admitted.

"I made fire! From the ring!" Denzel protested.

"After about twenty attempts," Samara said. "It's literally the most basic spell in existence. The average two-year-old can make it work by about their third try."

"You give fire rings to two-year-olds?" Denzel spluttered. "That sounds *very* irresponsible!"

The Elder woman's delicate features dipped into a frown. "Hmm. So no aptitude for either division. That is problematic," she said.

"I can teach him. We'll do extra work," Samara said.

"I'd be prepared to put in extra training also, ma'am," said Boyle, to Denzel's surprise. "If required. He could, I suppose, be a valuable asset to the team, and it would be a shame to lose—"

SPECTRE COLLECTORS

The Elder woman held up a hand for quiet. She spent several long seconds studying Denzel, before the silence was broken by Quinn pretending to be a tractor. "No. Kind as it is for you both to offer, he is neither a Vulteron nor an Oberon. That much is clear."

Denzel felt his heart drop into his stomach. "So... What are you saying? I have to go?"

"*We* have to *change*," said the Elder. "You have a gift, Denzel. A gift that, as far as I'm aware, no one else has ever had. You belong here. From this day forth, the Cult of Sh'grath will be split into three divisions, not two," she announced. "Vulteron. Oberon. And Denzel."

Denzel blinked. "Whoa. Really?"

"Really," said the Elder. Her smile flickered, just for a moment. "I mean, we might not stick with that name. It sounds pretty stupid alongside the other two, now that I say it out loud, but, you know, we'll come up with something."

She nodded at Denzel, Samara and Boyle in turn. "And now, we must depart. Rest assured, former Director Quinn shall be well taken care of."

"Great," said Denzel. "Thanks, and nice to meet you." He held a hand out to shake, but the Elder just glanced meaningfully at her sleeveless robe. "Oh, yeah, right," said Denzel, withdrawing his hand. He stepped back to let the Elder pass, then hesitated.

"Uh, before you go," he said. "Can I ask for one teensy little favour?"

Denzel sat in the front of the van, wedged between Boyle and the passenger door. Samara sat behind the wheel, watching him closely. "You sure about this?" she asked.

"Yes. No. Maybe," said Denzel. He inhaled deeply through his nose, then nodded. "Yes. I can do this."

"Want us to wait for you?" Boyle asked.

"Nah. It's fine," Denzel said. He opened the door and stepped out on to the street. "I'll see you back at base, OK?"

"OK," said Samara. "See you soon."

Denzel closed the door. Samara and Boyle both watched him as he walked along the road, his hands in his pockets. He stopped outside a gate, then turned and gave them a wave.

Samara started the engine. Denzel watched them pull away, then turned and gazed along the path to the front door of his house.

No, not his house. Not any more.

Slowly, he walked along the path, bouncing a finger along the fence like he'd done so many times before. He stopped when he reached the door. It took him quite a long time to raise his hand, and an even longer time to knock.

"I'll get it," shouted a voice from inside, and for a moment, Denzel thought about running. He stood his ground, though, and even managed a smile when Owen pulled open the door. "Hi," said Owen, before his face fell. "Wait, it's you. You're that kid from yesterday," he said.

"Yeah," Denzel began, but Owen's shouts drowned him out.

"Jack! Jack! That crazy kid from yesterday is here!"

"No, Owen, I'm not crazy," Denzel began. There was a commotion from behind Owen, and Jack appeared.

"Hey. It's you," said Jack.

Denzel nodded. "Yeah. It's me," he said, his throat tightening.

"What can we do for you?" Jack asked.

"Nothing," said Denzel, his voice barely a whisper. "That's why I came round. I just wanted to say that ... you don't need to worry. I'm OK."

Jack smiled. "Well, that's great to hear. Thank you for letting us know."

"No problem," said Denzel. He started to back away, then lunged forward and threw his arms around his dads. He hugged them, and neither of them pulled away, even though he held on until his arms began to ache.

At last, he stepped back. "Take care of each other," he said, wiping his eyes on his sleeve. He about-turned, and was halfway along the path before he turned back again. "Oh, and have you guys ever considered adopting?"

Jack and Owen glanced at each other. "We've thought about it," said Jack.

"Go for it," Denzel said. "You'll be amazing parents."

With that, Denzel turned and strode out of the garden.

The door closed behind him, and this time he didn't look back.

Denzel turned the corner at the end of the road, gave his eyes another wipe, then plonked himself down on a low wall.

"How was it?"

"About what you'd expect," said Denzel.

Smithy nodded. "Oh well," he said. "Least you've still got me."

Denzel laughed. "True. Still can't believe you turned down the Spectral Realm, though."

"Are you nuts?" said Smithy. "Did you see that giant monster thing? It would have eaten me alive!"

They stood up, shoved their hands in their pockets, then strolled in perfect time along the street. "Yeah, but you'd been searching for it for, like, hundreds of years," Denzel said. "And it was right there."

Smithy shrugged. "I was only searching because I was alone," he said. "And I'm not alone any more."

He turned so he was walking backwards ahead of Denzel. "So, it's official? We're really going to be Spectre Collectors?"

"I'm going to be a Spectre Collector," Denzel corrected. "The Elders said you could help out."

"Same thing," said Smithy.

"Not really," said Denzel.

"More or less," Smithy insisted.

"Well, less, certainly," Denzel replied.

Smithy turned and fell into step alongside Denzel again. "OK, here's one for you," he said.

"Go on."

"What would you rather fight, right? Fifty bears, all the size of chickens, or one chicken that's the size of a bear?"

Denzel laughed. "D'you know, Smithy?" he said, putting his arm around his friend's shoulders. "That is a very good question."

More funny fiction from Nosy Crow

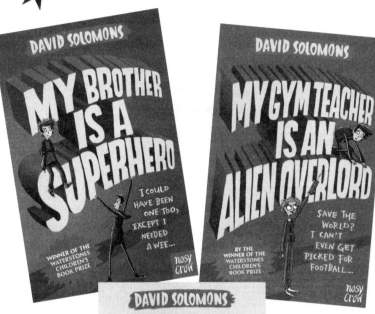